**Livia gave her line.
"Nothing seems right."**

Jonathan crossed the space between them. "We haven't much to be proud of, have we?"

"No." She studied his face, surprised at all the conflicting emotions she saw. What was acting and what was real, she wondered just before his lips touched hers.

She could feel the passion growing, and her lips parted under the pressure of his. There had never been anything like this, she thought breathlessly. Suddenly the play came back to her mind. She stiffened in his arms, feeling that he had caught her unawares and exposed her true feelings for him. Somehow, she had to stop it.

"You're not going to do that!" He said his line harshly, almost biting the words. Then he pulled her even closer, bending her body to his will.

D0830594

Books by Avery Thorne

HARLEQUIN PRESENTS
677—A SPLENDID PASSION
693—NO OTHER CHANCE

These books may be available at your local bookseller.

For a free catalog listing all titles currently available,
send your name and address to:

Harlequin Reader Service
P.O. Box 52040, Phoenix, AZ 85072-2040
Canadian address: Stratford, Ontario N5A 6W2

AVERY THORNE

no other chance

Harlequin Books

TORONTO • NEW YORK • LONDON
AMSTERDAM • PARIS • SYDNEY • HAMBURG
STOCKHOLM • ATHENS • TOKYO • MILAN

Harlequin Presents first edition May 1984
ISBN 0-373-10693-9

Original hardcover edition published in 1983
by Mills & Boon Limited

Copyright © 1983 by Avery Thorne. All rights reserved.
Philippine copyright 1983. Australian copyright 1983.
Except for use in any review, the reproduction or utilization of
this work in whole or in part in any form by any electronic,
mechanical or other means, now known or hereafter invented,
including xerography, photocopying and recording, or in any
information storage or retrieval system, is forbidden without
the permission of the publisher, Harlequin Enterprises Limited,
225 Duncan Mill Road, Don Mills, Ontario, Canada M3B 3K9.

All the characters in this book have no existence outside the
imagination of the author and have no relation whatsoever to
anyone bearing the same name or names. They are not even
distantly inspired by any individual known or unknown to the
author, and all the incidents are pure invention.

The Harlequin trademarks, consisting of the words
HARLEQUIN PRESENTS and the portrayal of a Harlequin,
are trademarks of Harlequin Enterprises Limited and are
registered in the Canada Trade Marks Office; the portrayal
of a Harlequin is registered in the United States Patent
and Trademark Office.

Printed in U.S.A.

CHAPTER ONE

SHE had expected, after her timid knock, that some sort of minor functionary would open the door. Instead, after a moment, she heard a voice—a rather well known voice at that—call out, 'It's open. Come in.'

She let herself in, expecting the grand entrance to have been accomplished, her particular god to be at last before her. A small foyer was a bit of a let-down. 'In here,' the voice prompted, and she followed obediently into a large and sunny sitting room. At this point she decided that nothing at all was going to be quite what she expected.

For no good reason she had expected the room to be dim and shadowy—probably because Jonathan Worth was a dramatic actor, much given to tragedies. He was also, according to the press, a night person. That, in itself, was not unusual among theatre people. But, if one could believe the press, his nights were wild and lively in the extreme; she hadn't expected him to function well at all in the bright light of day. Nor had she expected him to look quite so different from his stage persona. Lighting and make-up can do a lot for people, but it was surprising to see what they apparently did for Jonathan Worth. His face was all planes and angles and lines, similar to the face Livia had seen on stage, yet quite unlike it. On stage, the face seemed to have more flesh or substance to it; in person it seemed almost too vulnerable—too many lines, and the skin stretched too tautly across the bones beneath. 'Burned out' was perhaps too strong a characterisation, Livia decided. But 'well lived in' conveyed too little of what she saw.

'Livia Paige,' he said assessingly, without rising, and then gestured her into a chair facing his. 'I haven't seen you on the stage, I'm afraid, but I did see you in that movie—I forget the name. The one where you hung up the washing.'

Livia flushed slightly at his words. There was that one movie, in which she had, as he most succinctly put it, hung up the washing. That was about all she had done in the movie, other than appearing, looking trapped, at a suburban cocktail party. 'Most of me ended up on the cutting room floor,' she explained. 'Just as well, I expect.'

'Yes. First movies are notoriously unfair, as a general rule, especially if one's background is on the stage. Would you like coffee?'

She shook her head.

'Just as well. I haven't got any, at the moment.' He grinned engagingly, revealing a lighter soul beneath the planes and angles. 'Tell me something,' he leaned forward, deep blue eyes holding her fast, 'were you acting—I mean really acting—in that clothes line scene?'

It seemed to be a question of considerable significance, so she took her time in answering, remembering the scene. It had been shot outside, in a proper backyard borrowed for the occasion. She'd done nothing but hang clothes out on the line while pausing from time to time to watch trees blowing in the wind. The scene had been designed to indicate this particular housewife's desire for freedom. And she hadn't been acting at all. For the only time in the whole experience of shooting the film, she'd forgotten the corps of technicians watching her every move. She'd been completely lost in the feeling of the moment, working her way down the line, clothes pegs in hand, without a thought for movement or expression. It had been quite a nice piece of work—a daunting thought, when she knew she actually hadn't been acting at all.

And it seemed quite important to be honest with Jonathan Worth. If there was a chance that she might actually work with him, she ought to be completely honest. It was the only way to learn anything at all. On the other hand, if he had liked the scene, he might be less than impressed to learn that it bore no relation to the work she was capable of doing. There was a brief struggle in her mind before honesty won. 'No. I wasn't acting at all.'

He leaned back with a sigh of satisfaction. 'I thought not. At least I hoped not.' He smiled again, and Livia was fascinated at what it did to change him. Almost as an afterthought, she was pleased to have given the right answer.

'You see,' he was continuing, absently lighting a cigarette, 'it's my theory that at least a part of you has got to connect with the role you're playing. And in this thing I'm considering, it's absolutely vital that the woman be able to find some freedom—create it— within the limits of that god-awful life she's living. When Dickon approached me about the script, I liked the man's part. I've never played anyone quite so isolated.' He paused for a moment, eyes narrowed and staring off at some point beyond Livia. She decided that he looked quite isolated already.

'But Dickon said he wouldn't give me the script. If I wanted to do it, I'd have to do it here with the company. And, quite frankly, I didn't want to be lumbered with some cow of a woman who knew nothing about freedom, or space, or whatever you're going to make of the part.' Now his eyes were back to her, and she tried to answer his gaze without showing the selfconsciousness she felt. 'Dickon said he had someone who could do it—that you could do it. He told me that if I didn't believe him, I ought to look up that bit of rubbish Hollywood called a drama, and watch you at the clothes line. Which I did, and decided—well, the girl's got possibilities. You haven't had much to say, have you?' he enquired with a sudden switch.

'I haven't had much chance, have I?' It sounded more than a little rude to Livia's own ears, and it was not what she had intended to say. 'It seems to me,' she continued more carefully, 'that I can learn a great deal more by listening to you.'

'Oh God!' His expression was pained. 'You aren't going to get into that nonsense of worshipping at the shrine, are you?'

That cut so close to the bone that Livia felt the blood rush to her face. She had thought, as she neared the hotel, precisely that—that she was a worshipper approaching the shrine. She had gazed up at the grey façade of the building, soft and mellow against the brilliant blue of the autumn sky, and had told herself that behind one of those blank windows waited the god. Now she had a mental image of Jonathan Worth standing in a window, watching her approach and reading her mind. That thought left her feeling curiously exposed and defenceless.

He had seen the blush and spoke almost impatiently. 'Look, you're not some simpering adolescent, you know. Dickon says you're up to the part; in fact, he says you're rather good. Some idiot in Hollywood thought you could act, for whatever that's worth. You've been working in this business for some years now, I imagine, and you don't appear to be exactly starving.' At that point he eyed her appraisingly. Livia wasn't sure if he were assessing the cost of her clothes, or studying her figure. 'You haven't a reason in the world to think I know more about this business than you.'

'Oh yes, I do,' she shot back. 'I've seen you several times.'

He shook his head almost pityingly. 'My dear, do you have any idea how many actors I've seen at work? How many times I've told myself that I haven't a tenth of their talent?' He reached for another cigarette and grinned. 'Not too many, actually, but there have been a few. What's to make you think that you aren't one of those few? How do you know,' he demanded, drawing the words out for emphasis, 'how I felt when I watched that bit at the clothes line? For all you know, I decided that you've got more ability than I'll ever have—that you can do it with no effort at all, while I have to drag it out and fight to make it come out right.' He shook his head and continued in a milder tone, 'Look, love, I'm an actor, and you're an actor, and that makes us equals. And, for God's sake, don't just sit there and let me run on and on.'

'But you do it so awfully well. Run on, I mean.' Livia couldn't resist pointing that out to him.

'Oh, I'll be just as outrageous as people allow me to be. I'll dominate any conversation, so the trick is not to let me get out of control in the first place.'

'Well, that's fine for you to say. But greatness does intimidate people or at least the impression of greatness. Which isn't at all what I intended to say,' she added hastily, seeing the pained expression cross his face.

'Then what did you intend to say?' he asked silkily.

'I haven't the foggiest, at this point. I expect it must be quite a trick to keep you from getting out of control in the first place, and I've been at a considerable disadvantage ever since I walked through that door.'

'In what way?'

'I suppose that I expected meeting you to be a bit more formal. I thought you might want to have me read for you, or discuss the part, or something just a bit more structured. And I don't think you're being fair to expect a complete unknown to walk in off the street and treat you like an equal.' She saw the flicker of impatience in his face and hurried on, before he could interrupt again. 'It's all very well for you to be so democratic about our respective positions, but it's not terribly realistic. Perhaps I can be as good as you some day. But I'm not, yet. I haven't a tenth of your experience, and experience is the best teacher. Perhaps I have great potential, but—if you think that potential alone makes for great acting—I don't think quite as much of you as I thought I did.'

'Ah, that's a bit better.' Jonathan Worth nodded with a certain satisfaction. 'There are some tricks I can teach you. Every actor has his bag of tricks and can share them with others. For example——' he studied her consideringly for a moment, 'you have very nice hands, you know, and you use them very expressively and very gracefully. 'But, if you use them as much on the stage as you have here, you're going to have the audience watching them and not the rest of your character.'

Immediately Livia clasped her hands and forced them into her lap. 'My father always says that I can't talk without using them.'

'Well, the question is—can you act without them? Hold them in reserve so that they only appear when they need to, when they're going to add something. Too much of acting, today, is self-indulgence, when it ought to be discipline and economy. Only do a thing when it must be done. There's one little lesson in acting, if that's what you want from me.' He smiled more kindly. 'And I hope you won't persist in sitting on your hands in my presence—except when we're on stage. That's the whole point of acting—you can only use small parts of yourself in a role. A terribly self-effacing thing, acting is. To keep your sanity, you've *got* to be all of yourself, when you're not on stage.' He paused, looking momentarily lost. 'If, of course, you know what the hell yourself is.'

'And if you ever really stop acting,' Livia added.

He nodded, thoughtful for a moment. 'But let's not get into that one, right now. I left London at eight in the morning, which is two in the morning, over here. And it's what, now? About four? Wouldn't be so bad if I'd had a sensible night's sleep before I left, but there was a grand party— friends seeing me off, putting me on the plane. You get me on to a subject like when do we stop acting, at this point, and I'll make a perfect ass of myself. If I haven't already.' ·He rubbed one hand over his eyes and sighed.

'You haven't,' she said softly, feeling a pang, because he suddenly looked so terribly tired. 'Perhaps I ought to go now.'

He dismissed that thought with a wave of his hand. 'I'm going to the theatre to see you tonight. I must confess that I've forgotten what you're doing—if anyone bothered to tell me.'

'*Candida.*'

'And you are she?'

She nodded, and he narrowed his eyes, studying her face.

'You don't look old enough.'

'I'm not a girl any more,' she said sharply.

'Oh no, you're not a girl.' He grinned wickedly. 'Hardly that. Perhaps you were born old—some of us are. Why are you called Livia?' he enquired in another lightning shift of the conversation. 'Is it a stage name, or are you short for Olivia?'

'Neither. It's my own name. It was my great-grandmother's as well. Livia Chillingsworth Paige.'

'Good lord,' he said, his voice coloured with an amused sort of awe. 'Now that is a formidable thing. Livia · Chillingsworth Paige.' He shook his head. 'Imagine—a tiny baby lumbered with all that!'

'My mother believes in naming children so that it will look well if any of them ever write a book. Of course, she only had me, so she only got the one chance.'

'She wanted her child to be an author, did she?'

'I don't think so. She just liked names with some substance to them. Our whole family is filled with names of substance.'

'So—do you want to do this play with me?'

Livia tried to get her mind on to this new track. His thoughts seemed to skip so, like pebbles on smooth water. 'I'm not sure if you're offering it to me, or just asking for my feelings,' she said.

'Oh, I'm offering it to you, to whatever extent I'm in a position to offer it. Dickon wants you, and the other people in charge——' he gestured, sketching the image of a faceless group of business people, 'want Dickon's play done with me. So I suppose it doesn't matter whether I can offer it to you or not. If I don't say you can't, you've got it. And since I'd rather like to do it with you, the decision is yours.'

'Of course I want to do it.' Livia tried to keep her voice calm, to avoid showing the excitement building in her.

'Then you've got it, I guess. You see,' he continued carefully, 'I offer it to you now. That way, you don't have to go off to the theatre tonight and try to sell yourself to me through your performance.'

She hadn't thought of that, but he was quite right. If, after this afternoon's meeting, she hadn't had a decision from him, she'd have been playing directly to him, trying to convince him of her abilities.

'So tonight I can see the Candida you've been doing every other night?' he asked. 'You're not going to personalise the performance?'

Do I answer yes or not to that? she wondered wildly. 'I'll try to be the same,' she said finally.

'Oh lord, don't *try* anything. Do it! Did Lindbergh decide that he was going to *try* to fly the Atlantic? Trying gives one a possible out. Deciding to *do* something doesn't. You either do it, or you fail, and I have no patience with failure. And stop me now,' he added, his voice rising, 'before I go off on another sleepless philosophical binge.'

'All right, I will.' She smiled and stood up. 'I'll leave, because I wouldn't mind a little time to myself, before I go to work tonight.'

'That's better,' he observed approvingly. 'Quite different from the admiring little thing who walked in here a while ago. You've got the part, so you can be just as rude to me as you please.'

'I am never rude,' she retorted.

'Yes, that's probably true. I'll find out, won't I?' He rose from his chair and then stood eyeing her appraisingly. 'It's well that you're so small. It will add to the effect of repression when we do the play.'

Livia had never considered herself in the least small. She was relatively tall for a woman, but Jonathan Worth towered over her. Standing, he was a far more commanding figure, and she was glad he hadn't stood until this moment, now that the part was hers. He could have intimidated her with his sheer size, to say nothing of his reputation.

'Dickon's going to have a party after the performance tonight. You'll be there?' he asked, following her into the foyer.

'Yes, I expect so. But I shouldn't think you would, or do you never sleep?'

'Oh, I'll be much restored by tonight.' He grinned wickedly. 'Vast recuperative powers, and all that rot.' He extended his hand—she thought to shake hers, but instead he took her wrist and held it up. 'Straighten your fingers,' he directed, and she did so, her wrist still imprisoned in his grasp.

He studied her hand carefully, turning it first one way and then another. 'It's a nice hand,' he said finally. 'Large, but it's so long that it looks slender. If you must use them as much as you do, it's just as well that they're good ones.'

'I'm glad you approve,' she said, feeling more than a little foolish, standing there with her hand held up like a prizefighter's.

'Oh, I approve.' Several different emotions crossed his face so quickly that she couldn't read them, except for one, which appeared to be confusion. 'You'll do.' And then he released her, opened the door, and watched her go without another word.

CHAPTER TWO

LIVIA left the hotel in something of a daze, too preoccupied with what had just happened to be concerned with her surroundings. She'd met Jonathan Worth, and he wanted to work with her—although 'wanted' was perhaps too strong a word for it. 'Willing' might be more accurate. But it really didn't change the outcome; whether he wanted to, or was merely willing to, the fact remained that she was going to be working with Jonathan Worth.

The possibilities were endless, and each was more exciting than the last. As she made her way back to her apartment, she ran through them in her mind, savouring the special marvels of each. She had the leading female role in a new play of significance, and a leading man any actress would sell her soul to play opposite. There would be enormous publicity, thanks to the presence of Jonathan Worth in the production, and plenty of critical attention, too.

'Livia! Hey, Livy!'

Livia turned, suddenly aware that someone was calling her name. Behind her, running madly in an attempt to catch up was her friend and fellow tenant, Maureen Grenville.

'Why are you in such a hurry?' Maureen demanded, finally reaching her and pausing to catch her breath. 'I've been tearing after you for the last five minutes, trying to get your attention! I thought we could walk home together.' Then, giving a little more attention to Livia's expression, she asked, 'What happened, anyway? You look like you just won a million dollars.'

'It's nearly that good,' Livia said, feeling a little breathless herself. 'In fact, it's better. I've got the part!'

'What part?' Maureen asked. 'I didn't know you were trying for any part. And can we walk while you talk? I'm cold, even if you're not.'

'All right,' Livia agreed—she was prepared to agree with almost any suggestion at this point. 'And it's very difficult to explain. You see, Dickon has written this play——'

'Dickon is your producer or something?' Maureen asked vaguely, never having grasped the business complexities of the theatre. To her, acting was glamorous, and she didn't care to hear about the petty details of how the bills got paid.

'Dickon Stannard, he's the artistic director of the company,' Livia explained patiently. 'And he's also our angel, or main backer. And he's also a playwright, and he's written an absolutely smashing play.'

'How does he manage to do so many things?' Maureen asked with curiosity.

'He's independently wealthy,' said Livia with a smile. 'That helps a lot, if you want to be in the theatre. And he also has excellent taste, which is why he's the artistic director. He chooses the plays we'll do, and the directors, and things like that. And in his spare time he's a playwright, which is all that really matters at this point.

'I don't think I'm really following you,' Maureen observed as they entered the downstairs hall of their apartment house. 'Are we going to your place or mine?'

'Mine, if you don't mind. I've got to be thinking about getting ready for the theatre. And I told you it was difficult to explain,' Livia called over her shoulder as they went up the stairs. 'Dickon wrote this play, finally let some of us read it, and it really is a great play, with two very fat and juicy roles—one male and one female.' She paused for a moment at the top of the stairs and found her key. 'And once we'd read it,' she continued, letting them into her apartment, 'he just let it drop that Jonathan Worth is a friend of his, and that he'd also read the play and liked it and was willing to consider doing it with the company.'

'*The* Jonathan Worth?' Maureen demanded on an incredulous note. 'The real Jonathan Worth? You know someone who knows the real Jonathan Worth, and you never told me?'

'I never knew,' Livia said patiently, switching on the kitchen light and hunting for a can of soup. Fun as it was to tell someone her news, she still had to think about eating and getting to the theatre on time. 'Dickon is like that—he never has much to say about his personal life, and he certainly never brags about himself. Do you want some soup?' she added.

'I don't care about soup,' Maureen said impatiently. 'You suddenly, after all this time, tell me about an independently wealthy playwright *and* Jonathan Worth, and you expect me to think about soup! I don't see how you can either, at a time like this. You're going to do this play with Jonathan Worth, aren't you? That fat and juicy female role you just mentioned is the one you got today—right?'

'Right,' Livia agreed gravely, because the fact that she had the part suddenly seemed less pure excitement and more awesome responsibility.

'Well!' Maureen breathed, leaning against the kitchen wall. 'You're actually going to be acting with Jonathan Worth. Think of it!' She shook her head, obviously overcome with the wonder of it all. 'What happened? Did Dickon just tell you today?'

'It wasn't Dickon, actually,' Livia said carefully,

because the whole thing suddenly sounded too absurd. 'It was Jonathan Worth who told me.'

'*He* told you?' Maureen seemed able to leap like a mountain goat from one fresh peak of excitement to the next. 'You actually talked to him? You saw him?'

'Yes. That was the question, you see. I had to meet Jonathan Worth, to see if he approved of me. If he did, then he'd do the play, and I'd do it with him.'

'What's he like?' Maureen wanted instantly to know.

'Very strange,' said Livia, after a moment's thought. 'Much nicer, or kinder, than I'd expected him to be— and he'd absolutely hate it if he heard himself described that way.'

'Why?' Maureen asked, having settled down to watch Livia eat her supper and to hear some really fascinating gossip.

'I don't know. But he would.' Livia wondered on just what evidence she was basing this sudden conviction. 'He's also absolutely fascinating to listen to, when he gets wound up on acting.' Then she lapsed into silence, because there was far more to Jonathan Worth than that.

Something about him had caught her imagination: the lightning-swift changes in mood, perhaps, or the way he alternated between authority and charm. She played the significant moments over in her mind—the way he'd held her hand and studied it, the few flashes of wicked smile which made him look almost boyish. And—most of all, she realised suddenly—that moment when he'd said that he'd never played anyone so isolated before. It wasn't so much what he'd said—it was the look he'd had for just an instant, an arresting sense of isolation. She wondered why that had made such an impression.

'You're awfully far away,' Maureen said suddenly.

'I expect I am.' Livia laughed selfconsciously. 'It's a lot to absorb.'

'Isn't there anything more about Jonathan Worth?'

'Oh yes. He's quite disconcerting, because his mind skips around so. Just when I'd think I was following him, he'd jump to another subject and leave me trying to catch up. And he's a provocative person, too. He says things just for the effect, I think—says something outrageous and then waits to see what reaction he'll get. It's very strange.' She shook her head and finished her soup.

'What's very strange?'

'The fact that he's so nice, under all that other stuff. And very lonely, too, I think, but I don't think he'd want anyone to know that.'

'You do,' Maureen pointed out with logic.

'But I don't really. I'm just guessing.'

'Anyway, lonely doesn't exactly fit his image, or the publicity about him. Scads of women, my dear,' Maureen drawled, 'scads of women. And you're going to be the next one, Livy! Think of it.'

'Don't be silly,' Livia almost snapped, and wasn't sure why. 'I'm only going to work with him, after all.'

'Ah, but he always has romances with his leading ladies. Don't you know that, for heaven's sake?'

'I don't know anything about his personal life, if that's what you mean,' Livia answered with dignity.

'Well, it's not so very personal, which is something you'd know if you bothered with gossip columns. You'll find out, when you become the next,' she added with certain relish, following Livia down the narrow hallway to the bedroom.

'I am not going to become the next.'

'Of course you are,' said Maureen complacently. 'Why are you getting ready so early?' she asked, glancing at her watch.

'Because there's a party after the performance, only I'm not supposed to know about it yet. So I've got to find something that will look good but not so good that anyone can tell that I already knew about the party.'

'Of course—every girl must have a few of those kinds of outfits in her wardrobe. Just a little rag to wear to a party when you're pretending you don't know there's a party. Do you actors ever stop pretending?'

'I don't know,' Livia answered, suddenly struck. 'Jonathan Worth and I talked about that very thing this afternoon.'

'You can't go around calling him Jonathan Worth, all one word, if you're going to have an affair with him, you know,' Maureen said helpfully.

'I am not going to have an affair with him!' Livia cried, and pulled a random dress from the closet.

'Not that,' Maureen corrected, taking the dress from her hands and looking carefully through the closet. 'Here, wear this one. The colour is quite seasonal and it gives you a bit of a spark.' She handed Livia a dress of heavy linen weave, rust-coloured with soft golden embroidery around the neckline.

'Are you sure this doesn't look too partyish?' Livia asked uncertainly.

'The whole point is to look partyish, but this doesn't look too much so. I've seen you wear it to the theatre, even when you weren't planning to do anything afterwards. In fact, I think I've seen you wear just about everything you own to the theatre, because you don't own too awfully much, do you?'

'I can't afford too awfully much,' Livia admitted apologetically.

'I know. It's a funny thing, to be in such a glamorous profession and not be able to afford to look glamorous. All of which will change, now that you're going to act with Jonathan Worth. Which is just as well,' Maureen continued, examining Livia's dresses and obviously finding all of them less than satisfactory. 'You really don't have anything that fits the image of what a girl having an affair with Jonathan Worth would wear.'

'Will you please stop talking about my having an affair with Jonathan Worth?' Livia commanded. 'Why don't *you* have the affair with him?'

'I'd love to,' Maureen agreed with an impish smile. 'But I don't expect he'd want to have an affair with me. We have nothing in common.'

'I don't think we'll have much in common, except acting,' Livia observed, struggling with the zipper on her dress, 'if what you say is true.'

'Oh, I know,' Maureen agreed loftily. 'On the surface, it would appear so. But I have a theory about you and Jonathan Worth. You see, you're a very sensible and steady person, in spite of the fact that you're an actress, and actresses aren't supposed to be like that. And you're just what someone like Jonathan Worth has been looking for, for all these years. A truly *good woman*, one who will love him for himself, and not for his fame and money,' she finished in fine overworked dramatic style.

'And you're an incurable romantic,' said Livia, laughing as she hastily ran a comb through her hair.

'I know,' Maureen agreed solemnly. 'It's too depressing, because I never have any good material to work with. But now I do! Think of it—Jonathan Worth and Livia Paige, stars of stage, screen and television, together at last! And besides,' she added, 'your names sound well together. They both have a certain stature, or something. And Livia Worth sounds awfully good, too, although I expect you couldn't use it professionally. And you probably won't ever get that name, because he is *not* the marrying type.'

'And I am not the type to marry him,' Livia said tartly, grabbing her bag and heading for the door. 'And certainly not the type to have an affair with him!'

'You aren't the type to have an affair with anyone,' Maureen said flatly, following in Livia's wake. 'But if anyone can change you, he can.'

'Out!' said Livia forcefully.

'I know, I'm going. But you're protesting too much, you know.'

'I don't know,' Livia snapped, allowing Maureen to precede her down the stairs. 'I just think you're being silly. It is not a case of protesting too much; it's just that I have no intention of having an affair with that man.'

'So you say,' Maureen agreed, stopping on the second floor landing and unlocking the door to her own apartment. 'But you're already partly caught, you realise. You told me that he's nice and kind, which is not the way most people would describe him. And then you decided that he's lonely, which is not the way *anyone* would describe him. So you're giving him a lot of original thought, which means that you're already partly hooked!' she called after Livia's retreating figure.

After the session with Maureen, Livia found all the talk at the theatre about Jonathan Worth to be more than she wanted to hear. Most of the company had known that he was coming to Boston to discuss the play with Dickon. No one knew what he had decided about it and rumours spread, each varying according to its source. Livia felt that she ought not to mention her visit, or the seeming certainty that he was going to do the play. So gossip continued until the curtain, with the general consensus being that Dickon would not have laid on a party if Jonathan Worth had not agreed to do the role. That comforting supposition made for a general high among the members of the cast, and the performance went well. Everyone was aware that Jonathan Worth was in the house, sitting in the fourth row. (Someone had looked out to check.) His presence removed any tendency to staleness which might have begun to creep in after almost four weeks of doing the same thing.

After the performance, Livia listened to more backstage chatter as she sat quietly and alone in her dressing room. The pitch was higher, people acutely aware that they were about to see, and be seen by, Jonathan Worth. She could tell, from the sounds, that the rest were hurrying to be off to Dickon's. She ought to get moving, she told herself. If she didn't, she'd be the last one out and would have to take a cab alone, an expense she would prefer to avoid. Still, she felt curiously unwilling to move, and didn't, until she heard a soft tap on her door.

'Come in,' she called, reaching for a tissue to begin to take off her make-up.

It was Perry Adams, the young man who played the poet to Livia's Candida. 'Aren't you coming to the party?' he asked, seeing that she had got exactly nowhere in the changing process.

'Oh yes. I'm just a little slow tonight.'

'A little more Candida than you could handle? You were awfully good tonight, Livy. I guess we all were. Nothing like knowing the great man is out there, to perk up the performance.' He leaned comfortably against the door frame, already out of make-up and back into street clothes.

'I thought so,' Livia agreed, working more swiftly at

her make-up. 'I'm going to have to make you leave in a minute,' she added, moving over to the little sink.

'I'll wait for you. The others are sorting themselves out, getting ready to leave. I'll even spring for the cab. After all, I'll be treating a star about to be born.'

'That's rubbish, Perry, and you know it.'

'Not a bit, Livy. It stands to reason—he's going to take the part, and you're going to play opposite him. The whole world will come to see it and discover just how good you are. And then, when you're famous, you'll remember my generosity, and find the perfect part for me.'

'Do shut up, Perry,' said Livia with some heat, because part of what he'd said was a bit too much like what she had been thinking herself. 'Go stand in the hall while I change, and we'll share the cab fare.'

He went out obediently, and she changed quickly, still taking the time to hang her costume carefully for the next night's performance. By the time she emerged the place had completely cleared out except for Perry, waiting patiently in the hall.

'You'll be able to make an entrance,' he observed. 'And I shall bask in the reflected glory.' And then, seeing her expression, he added in a more conciliatory tone, 'I know, Livy—you really aren't playing that game. But can't I tease my big sister just a bit?'

And she softened, because he was so like the little brother she'd never had. They had a running joke about it because, while he was only three years younger, he seemed so very young to her. 'Puppy,' she called him sometimes, and he would assume a begging posture, looking up at her with eager puppy eyes. Livy knew that he loved her in his fashion, because he was as caught up in his role as the adoring poet as she was in hers, as the object of his affection.

Together they walked to the end of the alley, where Perry finally managed to hail a cab.

'It can't be too easy for you,' Perry began, after giving Dickon's address to the driver. 'Do you still feel on tenterhooks about it, or do you think it's settled?'

'I think it's settled,' she said, almost in a whisper, because to admit it might make it go wrong.

'It could change your whole life,' Perry observed. 'I know I was kidding you, back at the theatre, but it's really not a joke. You're awfully good, Livy. I've often wondered why you didn't stay in New York and keep plugging away. I really felt you'd have made it, if you'd stayed. And there didn't seem to be any real future here in Boston—not in the way you seemed to be settling in, anyway.'

'I know. I explained it to myself by saying that I'd rather act in good material, with a good company, and not waste my time on uncertainties, waiting for the big break.'

'Maybe what you've been doing here is the right way. You've certainly learned a lot—I think you've grown a lot, doing the repertory stuff. Maybe you gave yourself a lot better chance at being an out-and-out star by coming back here and really learning your craft.'

'Maybe.' She sounded uncertain, unconvinced, and she saw Perry's curious glance in the headlight glare of an oncoming car. 'But maybe I didn't want the big break, Perry. Maybe I don't really want to be a star. Maybe I just want to stay here, in this happy little company, and be normal.'

'Oh, Livy, it's a backwater!' He patted her hand comfortingly. 'You really have it. You shouldn't spend your life here, when there's so much more you could do.'

'I don't know. I think I'm afraid of it. Part of me wants it so much. Just talking to Jonathan Worth was exciting—and thinking about working with him is so much more——' She shook her head, trying to find the words. 'I want to do it, but it frightens me. It could change my whole world.'

She shivered suddenly, filled with a feeling of presentiment. It was going to happen, and it was going to change her whole world. It was going to happen, and she would never be the same again. And then, in an effort to shake off that heavy, frightening knowledge, she laughed. 'It's so silly, Perry. Here I am, worrying about being a star when it hasn't even happened yet. And, the way things go in this business, it isn't going to happen. If we do it, Jonathan Worth will dominate the stage and completely overshadow me. Afterwards, people will say, "Oh, yes, that play Jonathan Worth did in Boston. Who was that little thing who played the woman?" ' She brought one hand up to sketch a flat denial in the air. 'No one gets noticed when Jonathan Worth is dominating the stage.'

Jonathan Worth was certainly dominating the stage when Livia and Perry arrived at the party. He was standing in the centre of the large room, glass in hand, while the others clustered around him. A few of the least important members of the company had retreated to chairs or the couch, but every eye was on Jonathan Worth. That wasn't difficult, because he loomed taller than anyone else in the room. Only Dickon seemed removed from the activity. With no expression on his face, he was sitting on a high stool against the far wall, watching the whole production. He noticed Livia and Perry as they entered the room, but acknowledged their presence with only the smallest of nods. No one else had eyes for them, so they stood unnoticed in the shadowy doorway.

Jonathan Worth was expounding on some subject— Livia didn't know what, having come in at the middle of the story. 'It was incredibly bad,' he was exclaiming, his voice large and resonant in the room. 'They hadn't the least idea of what they ought to be doing and, as a consequence, they did nothing at all. And I said——' He paused and bent down to grind out the stub of his cigarette. As his head came up again, his eyes met Livia's. He missed just a beat and then grinned. 'I said a lot of rubbish which isn't worth repeating—particularly now.' He pointed to Livia, a sweeping, theatrical gesture followed by all eyes. 'Candida has arrived. She chose the one who needed her more. A brilliant performance.' And then he bowed to her while the others murmured appreciatively, something they wouldn't have thought of doing without the benefit of his theatrics.

Is he drunk already? Livia wondered with dismay. He's behaving outrageously and placing me in an outrageous position. And she could only suffer in silence as he crossed the room, took her hand, and led her passively back to the centre of the group.

'Now——' he began, pausing only long enough to finish his drink. 'Now is the time for the announcement, although I don't suppose there's any point to it. You all know what it's going to be anyway. But indulge me just a bit. I'm going to be leaving the vainglorious world behind for a few months—which is to say that I shall be working for nothing, or so nearly nothing as to be nothing, given my life style. So you must all allow me this piquant and totally unnecessary gesture. Dickon.' He turned to where Dickon still sat composedly against the wall. 'For God's sake, get your old friend a drink, and bring one for yourself as well.'

And, while Dickon impassively complied with the command, Jonathan Worth turned back to the assembled group, while Livia suffered silently beside him.

'I shall get to know you all better in the months to come—but of course you aren't supposed to know that yet. However, I watched your work tonight, and it was quality work. Not all of you were on the stage, but the quality was there—in the set, in the lighting. It was a damned fine piece of work.' He might be drunk, Livia decided, noting dispassionately that he was still holding her hand, but he was giving them what they were longing to hear. For once they had been noticed by one who really mattered in the theatre and that, plus the promise of more to come, held them spellbound.

And now the group parted to allow Dickon access. He was juggling three glasses, and there was a bit of anticlimactic business while he passed one to Livia and another to Jonathan. And Jonathan, who had not looked at Livia at all since leading her into the group, now turned to stare at her. She sensed enquiry, uncertainty, almost apology, in his gaze, but it was just a fragment before he turned back to the rest.

'The announcement I have to make—not that I need to—is that Dickon has written what I consider to be a great play.' He smiled affectionately down at his friend. 'Not, perhaps, a play for the ages, but certainly a play for this age. It deserves notice and critical consideration. And I am prepared to do my humble best——' here he smiled that wicked grin that Livia had already seen—— '—to see that notice and critical consideration are forthcoming. I shall be the man in Dickon's play, and Livia Chillingsworth Paige, whom you all know and, I trust, respect as you should, will be the woman.'

There was a small round of applause and, Livia sensed, a collective sigh of relief. It was at last official; unbelievable good fortune had touched them all.

'I would be more specific, but Dickon, in his infinite wisdom, has seen fit to give me no name but—"the man". And poor Livia here, whose own name rings with such substance——' He shot her a quick look of satisfaction, obviously remembering her words of the afternoon. She decided that perhaps he wasn't quite so drunk as he appeared to be. 'Livia must be content to be "the woman". Dickon has obviously written a feminist play, and Livia and I must serve as symbols.'

'Not feminist, Jon,' Dickon corrected quietly. 'Humanist.'

'I stand corrected. Dickon says it's humanist, so humanist it must be. So, shall we drink to humanism and to a critical success?'

The group drank obediently. Then, as Jonathan turned away, still holding Livia's hand, general conversation started up as though to fill the vacuum left behind. He moved her a few paces away from the rest and then released her hand and turned to face her.

'Now,' he began, 'before we go any further, wouldn't you remove that disapproving look from your face?'

'I'm sorry, but I'm not very good at grand gestures. They make me uncomfortable.'

'Well, lord knows they're not always to my liking, either. But they're sometimes necessary. It seemed to me that this group needed one tonight. You've all been doing fine work, with precious little recognition, according to Dickon. And, to be completely objective about myself, I offer them—and you—a chance for considerable recognition. Is it so terribly wrong to offer it all nicely wrapped up, with a bright bow?'

'No, I suppose it isn't.'

'You know, I'm not always allowed to be what I want to be,' he told her. 'People expect a certain level of behaviour from me, and I let them down if I don't come through.' He extracted a pack of cigarettes from his pocket and lit one, looking suddenly weary. 'But I'm not sure just how much longer I can keep it up. So couldn't you appear to monopolise me for just a few minutes? Give me a chance to recharge.'

'What do you want me to do, exactly?' asked Livia.

'Gesture me to that bench over there, sit down beside me, and talk a blue streak, while I appear to listen with rapt attention. Don't expect me to answer, and if you actually want me to hear what you have to say, remember to tell it all to me later, because I'm probably not going to hear a blessed word you're saying.'

She nodded and did exactly as he had directed, except for asking one question before proceeding. 'Have you slept at all yet?'

'For about an hour after you left. Now, for God's sake, just talk and leave me in peace for a few minutes.' He leaned one arm against the back of the bench, resting his chin on his hand, the cigarette burning forgotten. As she began to talk, the look he gave her was one of complete absorption, but his eyes were far away, staring somewhere beyond her.

'I don't believe you've had anything to drink tonight,' she began, taking him at his word. 'I expect it's tea or ginger ale, and just a part of the act. I thought you were drunk as a lord when I first came in, but you aren't. You look tired to death right now.' She wondered if she ought to be so personal, but he had said he wouldn't hear a thing and he certainly didn't appear to; nothing was registering at all. 'It's strange, because you didn't look tired at all while you were

holding forth. I'd like to know how you manage that—
not to look tired, when you are. I also think,' she
continued, warming to the subject, 'that you're an
awful fool to be burning the candle quite so vigorously
at both ends. You either shouldn't have stayed up all
night in London, or you shouldn't have allowed
Dickon to have this party for you tonight. And even if
you aren't drinking anything but weak tea—which
your liver must appreciate—you ought to be getting
more rest. Now, I've said all that and I suppose I
shouldn't have, except that you're not hearing me.
And I sound like your mother, or a nagging wife,
which wasn't my intention. I actually didn't have any
intentions, except to keep talking, and I seem to be
running out of things to say. Perhaps I shall now
quote some poetry to you, or give you some selections
from Shakespeare, and that will pass as a reading, to
give you some idea of my range or whatever. The only
trouble is that the only blocks of Shakespeare I know
are from the men's roles, because those are the ones I
like best. I always resent being a woman when I read
Shakespeare, because all the best roles are for the men.
Which isn't strictly true, because there are a few good
parts for women. But not enough, which is quite
unfair. You know, they're going to think we're starting
an affair over here.' She paused and deftly removed
the burned-out cigarette from between his fingers.

'I'm not sure just how I'm going to live this down,'
she went on. 'They'll all think I'm a snob for
monopolising you, and they'll wonder just what it was
I had to say that you found so fascinating. They'll all
begin to gossip and when you come back to start
rehearsing, they'll all be watching for signs of a
blooming romance.'

'They'll probably see some, too,' he said so
unexpectedly that she jumped. 'You're a love and

you've probably just saved my life—or at least my reputation.'

'I didn't know you were back,' she said.

'I haven't been for too long. You needn't worry—whatever rot it was you were saying to me, I didn't hear a bit of it.'

'That's just as well,' she murmured, and he looked at her with a gentle smile.

'That sounds interesting. I wonder what I missed.' And then, while he fished for another cigarette and went through the business of getting it lit, Livia studied his face with less objectivity and more affection than she had that afternoon.

It was a strong face and a very attractive face, although not conventionally handsome. It was too thin and too well used to be precisely handsome. The absolutely fascinating thing was the way emotions and thoughts flickered across it. It had to be one of the most expressive faces she had ever seen. She had the sudden thought that he must be forced to act all the time, to guard against revealing everything to anyone who cared to look. Unless, of course, not everyone could read his face as she could. But she put that thought away quickly. It was likely to lead to other, even deeper, thoughts.

'I suppose I ought to mingle,' he said after a silence.

'Yes, and so should I. I want to thank Dickon for the chance he's giving me. And I have to give Perry my half of the cab fare.'

'Perry? The poet—yes? He shows some promise, I think.'

'Really? May I tell him? He'd be so pleased to hear that you think so.'

'Why not, if I don't get to him first. I'm about to go back into my act, Livia dear. Try not to look so disapproving this time, will you?'

And then Jonathan Worth pulled her to her feet
and, after touching her lightly on the shoulder, was off
into the crowd of people, looking strong and vigorous
and very much the life of the party. Livia watched him
for a few minutes as he moved from person to person,
leaning down to catch their words, speaking seriously
and then laughing, as though the whole thing were a
joke and he knew it. It was disturbing to watch,
somehow. She wondered why he simply couldn't
announce that he was tired and was going back to his
hotel and sleep. What, exactly, did he think he owed
all these people? But she didn't get any farther with
that thought, because Dickon was suddenly beside
her.

'Well, what do you think of him?' he asked quietly.

'I'm not quite sure. He's a mass of contradictions,
isn't he?'

'Always has been, at least as long as I've known
him, and we go back quite a few years. You two
seemed to have a lot to talk about just now.' Livia was
still trying to form a suitable reply when Dickon
added, 'Or else you were simply giving him time to
recharge—that's what he calls it.'

'Does it happen very often?'

'Oh yes, the last few years at least. We're none of us
getting any younger, but he feels that he mustn't
change.'

Livia nodded absently, following Jonathan's figure
as it moved around the room. 'You two were at school
together?'

'Yes. In prep school, and then we both went on to
the drama school at North-western. It's an old
friendship.'

Livia compared the two men in her mind. It seemed
strange to think of them as being approximately the
same age. Superficially, Dickon seemed much the

older, with hair receding and waistline thickening. But their faces reversed the impression, because Dickon's was relatively untouched by time—well rounded and unlined. Even stranger to think of them as friends, except that opposites do attract. No two people could be more opposite than Dickon Stannard and Jonathan Worth.

'You know,' she began, changing the subject because she simply couldn't dwell on Jonathan Worth indefinitely, 'I haven't begun to properly thank you for what you're doing for me.'

'You don't need to. It was a treat to write that play, with you in my mind.'

'Was I?' That somehow made it even more of a gift.

'Oh yes. I started it last year, after I'd got to know you. You have fascinating reserves, Livy, and I wanted to give you a chance to show them. I also thought that a woman like you was worth committing to paper.'

'I feel terribly selfconscious,' she confessed.

'You shouldn't. I had you both in mind.' His eyes were following Jonathan. 'I've known for years how to write him, but I couldn't find the conflict until I got to know you.'

'Do you really mean conflict?' Livia asked.

'Of course.' Dickon sounded quite pleased. 'It's an issue of dominance, of seeing which of you is the stronger.'

'There shouldn't be any question about that!'

'You're putting your money on Jon?' Dickon asked.

'Naturally.' She wondered how there could be any question about that.

'I think you might be wrong,' he told her. 'You've got all kinds of reserves, so you don't need to control people. Your strength is built in, not added on. But Jon is really very fragile, although most people don't see it because he's got such a marvellous ability to control situations. He uses people; he manipulates them, or bends them to suit his purpose. He must have people behave as he wishes—it's the only way he can protect himself. If you're not careful, Livy, he'll use you, as he uses everyone. And, for some reason I don't quite understand, I think he could hurt you very badly in the process.'

'I don't agree,' she said firmly, and wondered why.

'I hope I'm wrong. But I have wondered sometimes if I've done the right thing in bringing the two of you together like this. I've been selfish because I want to write a great play and there's great potential in pitting the two of you, as characters, against one another. And I think that with the two of you doing it, it will be great. It's going to create problems for anyone else who ever tries to do the play, because it will never work as well again. It belongs to the two of you. But it isn't going to be easy for you, Livy. Don't thank me yet. Wait until it's over and see if you really want to.'

He was being so serious, Livia thought with impatience. Surely he was dramatising too much. Of course it wasn't going to be easy. She hadn't expected acting with someone as demanding of excellence as Jonathan Worth to be easy. And the role wasn't going to be easy, either. It might have been written for her, but she wasn't the woman. She was someone else entirely, although she and the woman had certain shared characteristics. She was going to have to work awfully hard to bring out all the things required by the part.

And Jonathan? she wondered. She supposed she could become involved with him, if the possibility presented itself. Right now, though, it didn't look too likely. He was flirting outrageously with Honey Pressman, the newest member of the company. Honey

was fresh out of school and looked it, Livia thought
with a sigh. No lines at all, on that face. Eight years
did make a difference; twenty-nine could not be
twenty-one again. And yet Honey had remarkable
talent, the ability to be all dewy-eyed innocence one
minute and evil incarnate the next. A useful member
of the company, because she was so versatile. And
apparently, at this moment, a useful addition to
Jonathan's circle of friends.

'Perhaps you should be worrying about Honey,'
Livia observed to Dickon almost waspishly, but he
merely smiled.

'Oh no, Honey can take care of herself. She knows
exactly where she's going.'

'To bed with Jonathan,' Livia said tartly.

Dickon laughed out loud at that. 'Oh, Livy, be
careful! You aren't going to find this easy at all. And
let me get you another drink. You're going to need it
before this night is over.'

Perhaps Dickon was a closet sadist, Livia thought,
as she began to circulate. He'd said just enough to
make her wonder and speculate about herself and
Jonathan. About herself *and* about Jonathan, she
corrected. There didn't seem to be much point in
speculating about herself and Jonathan—Honey
seemed to have things pretty well sewed up in that
department.

Livia chatted with first one member of the group
and then another, agreeing that the new play was an
exciting thing, agreeing that Jonathan Worth was
going to do great things for the company, modestly
accepting compliments on her own part in the
production. And all the while she was aware that the
people talking to her would far rather have been
talking to Jonathan Worth. They all knew her—'good
old Livy'—and Jonathan was the dazzler, the knight

on the white charger who was riding in to rescue them all. No one wanted to talk to Livia with much concentration, because there was always the possibility that they might miss a chance to talk to Jonathan instead.

And Jonathan was certainly circulating most assiduously, even though his progress was somewhat hampered by Honey, who had herself well wrapped around one arm of the great man. It meant, Livia noted sardonically, that he could smoke or drink, but could not do both at once. Not that it seemed to bother him; he appeared prepared to sacrifice one of his other two vices for Honey. He divided his time pretty equally between Honey and whomever he included in the conversation. But the two of them were exchanging meaningful glances, and there were moments when they stared soulfully into each other's eyes, oblivious to those around them. It looked more than promising for Honey. Livia might have the part, but Honey was going to have the space in the gossip columns. Not that Livia wanted anything to do with that sort of thing, she told herself hastily.

The hours wore on and no one showed any signs of leaving, or of even wanting to leave. No doubt that was because Jonathan showed no sign of wanting to leave, and no one wanted to leave while there was still a chance of talking one last time with him. There was a limit to the amount of circulating anyone could do, and some people were finally drawn to Dickon's piano, where he played show tunes as though he made his living as a cocktail lounge pianist. Jonathan and Honey were conspicuously not a part of that group, and Livia was just as conspicuously a member of it. She had curled up in a corner of Dickon's leather couch, wondering why she at least didn't have the courage to leave the party. She'd had quite enough of

Jonathan Worth for one day, and she'd have a good
deal more before the play was over. Still, it would be
interesting to see if Honey accomplished her purpose.
Livia decided that she'd rather see it happen than
listen to endless gossip about it the next evening at the
theatre.

So she stayed, eyes closed most of the time,
listening to Dickon's gentle playing and the voices—
some singing, some still in conversation—all of
it occasionally punctuated by Jonathan's laugh.
Because her eyes were closed, she didn't see Honey
untangle herself from Jonathan's arm long enough to
freshen her make-up. Nor did she see Jonathan's
quick whispered conversation with Dickon, nor
Dickon's quiet nod. She opened her eyes only when
Dickon stopped playing in the middle of a song and
announced that his fingers were too tired to play any
longer and that he, at least, was going to move
around.

As though on cue, Jonathan settled himself near
Livia on the couch, long legs stretched out. 'Dickon
may do all the moving about he pleases,' he announced
to the room at large. 'I've done my share.' He made a
business of lighting yet another cigarette and then
leaned back, staring up at the ceiling, or at nothing.
'What's the time, Livia?' he asked after a silence.

'I shouldn't think it would matter to you,' she
observed.

'Oh, it doesn't, actually. It was just a gambit, a way
to open the conversation. I have the feeling that you're
out of charity with me.'

'I can't imagine why.'

'You can't? Well, I can. I told you that I was about
to go back into my act. Now it seems that you either
forgot or didn't believe me. Which is a pity, because I
ought to get a bloody Oscar for this night's work. And

I've done it all for you, love, in case you've forgotten
that as well.'

'I haven't the slightest idea what you're talking
about,' she told him, and meant it.

'You were afraid the whole group would think you a
snob for monopolising me. So I made damn well sure
they didn't. And if you think that God knows how
long with Honey is my idea of fun you've read me very
wrong.'

'It certainly looked like fun,' Livia said silkily, and
he grinned.

'That's the spirit, Livia! Are you ready to leave?'

'Wouldn't it be more to the point to see if Honey is
ready to leave?'

'No, it would not. I planned to leave with you and,
if anything, Honey has strengthened my resolve.
Perhaps I forgot to mention that to you.'

'Perhaps you did.'

'Oh, for God's sake, Livia, do have a heart!' he
sighed. 'It's been a long day or two or three, or
whatever it's getting to be by now.'

'How do you propose to leave Honey behind?' Livia
asked with some interest.

'Very simple, love. We get up and walk out. Honey
is, at the moment, deep in conversation with Dickon—
discussing her role in this grand new play. She'd much
rather leave with me, but she can hardly afford to be
rude to the playwright and principal backer of the
company. Honey, as you may have noticed, is well
aware of priorities. And while I may be her main
ambition, she can't be sure of me until the play goes
on. And she'll not be here when the play goes on if she
isn't nice to good old Dickon—while you and I walk
out the door. Now, will you please stand up and
walk—I seem constantly to be giving you stage
directions—while I shamble behind, looking decidedly

the worse for wear and unlikely to try anything in the least improper.' He smiled appealingly at her and her resolve broke.

'All right. You do look like death,' she admitted.

'And feel even worse, if such a thing is possible. I'm not as young as I used to be.'

'That's what Dickon said earlier.'

'About himself, or about me?' he asked with a degree of interest.

'About you.'

'Oh lord, has Dickon been talking rubbish about me again?' Jonathan seemed suddenly restless, almost on edge. 'I wish he wouldn't. Dickon has some strange ideas about me.'

But Livia wasn't sure if he was saying that for her benefit or his own.

Outside, dawn was beginning to streak the sky and Jonathan paused on the steps, shaking his head ruefully. 'I really should stop this nonsense, shouldn't I? The fresh air feels good. Can we walk to your place from here?'

'I think we'll have to, unless you want to go back in and brave Honey, while you call for a cab. It's about a half hour's walk, or less if you're prepared to cross the Common and risk a mugging.'

'I need to walk and hear nothing at all—not one single voice—for just a little while. That is, if you don't mind.'

'I don't.'

'That's good.' He smiled and took her arm and they started off, climbing back up to the top of Beacon Hill before starting down the other side.

Their footsteps echoed on the quiet street, his sounding slow and almost dragging, hers quicker as she worked to keep up with his long stride. There was a cool breeze and Livia lifted her face to it. Beside her, Jonathan's head was bent, as though he wanted to see each step, study it intently.

Livia felt the strangeness of the moment. If someone had told her a day ago that she would be walking home in the early morning with Jonathan Worth, she would have found it hard to believe. Not absolutely impossible, because there was a small part of Livia which believed that great and unusual things could happen to her. And surely walking home in the early dawn, her arm tucked firmly in that of Jonathan Worth, was great and unusual—or perhaps it was merely unusual, with nothing great about it. The great thing would be the chance to play opposite him in Dickon's new play.

This moment certainly was strange, and Livia had conflicting feelings about herself and Jonathan Worth among the blank and sleeping buildings. There was nothing in the least companionable about their being together on the lonely street. Although he held her arm, she felt no sense of contact between them. He was totally absorbed, totally withdrawn from her. What was it that Dickon had said? That Jonathan was very open about everything except himself. Dickon was wrong, she decided, because Jonathan wasn't being open about anything at all right now. And, looking back over the evening, she wondered if he actually had been at all open. He'd been expansive, occasionally outrageous, certainly highly verbal. But it seemed, in retrospect, like a gigantic defence. He had dominated each exchange, controlled everything about himself and those to whom he'd spoken.

That seemed to confirm what he had said, in the hotel room—that he would be outrageous and dominate, and the trick was not to let him get out of control in the first place. Perhaps that was the only real thing he had said about himself. Thinking back over the evening's performance (because there didn't seem to be any other way to characterise his behaviour) Livia wondered if there hadn't been a warning, or even a plea, in what he had said that afternoon. Did he want to be controlled? That was a bit of a mind-boggler, because she couldn't see how anyone could control a personality as forceful as his. And it seemed more than a little presumptuous to be thinking such thoughts. She'd known him—if, indeed, she knew him at all—for less than twenty-four hours, and here she was, wondering about controlling him.

And yet it was hard not to think thoughts like those. He was such an incredible force; he'd hit her square between the eyes, so to speak. Never before had she met anyone even remotely like him. Dickon was right about one thing: he was fragile. She'd sensed that from the very first. It was that combination of fragility and force which had caught her imagination. He was totally captivating, he took her breath away, and much of the reason for that was that he was such an open contradiction. Dickon had said that he used people. Perhaps that was true, but it seemed as likely that people would want to be used by him, would allow themselves to be used by him, without any conscious effort on his part.

All of which seemed terribly muddled to Livia— muddled and inconclusive. But being muddled was hardly surprising, given the fact that she'd been up almost twenty-four hours now. Her mind had a tendency to go revolving off on pointless thoughts, when she was very tired. But, if she was tired, how much more tired must he be? She tried to work it out, approximately, in her mind. It must be about six now, which made it noon in London. On noon of the previous day, London time, he'd already left, having partied all the previous night. Perhaps he'd slept late, the day before that—what? two days ago. That seemed to make it forty-eight hours without sleep for him. Except for an hour's nap last evening, and perhaps some additional time on the plane.

How did he do it? she wondered. If she was getting muddled after twenty-four hours, how did Jonathan manage after twice as long? She turned to look at him and his eyes came back from somewhere, far away, to meet hers.

'Am I going too fast for you?' he asked with a crooked smile.

'Well,' she said consideringly, 'it's not quite so bad as it was at the party.'

'A loaded comment. I'm not sure just how to approach it.'

'You don't have to approach it at all.' And, since he seemed disposed to talk now, she continued, 'I was trying to work out just how long you've been up, and forty-eight hours seems about right.'

'I don't keep track of things like that.'

'I'm sure you don't, but that wasn't my point. I meant that you needn't make anything of what I say, after two days without any sleep.'

'You're going to humour me, then?'

'Not humour you, precisely, just not expect anything of you. Cosset you, perhaps.'

'Cosset me.' He smiled the crooked smile again. 'Now there's a fine old word! I shouldn't mind being cosseted just a bit, right now. Would you consider cosseting me with a cup of strong black coffee when we get to your apartment? And I hope we do get to your apartment soon, because I'm suddenly feeling rather ragged.'

'It's only about five minutes. And I could cosset you with coffee and bacon and eggs, if you like.'

'That would be nice. The problem with these long nights is that they leave me with an appetite. And in a strange city, I'm usually reduced to all-night diners, and such places depress me. Filled with lonely people, sad and shabby people. I find it uncomfortably close to the truth.'

'But you're not shabby,' Livia pointed out, and he grinned.

'I notice that you carefully avoided sad and lonely. You can be quite perceptive when I give you the chance.'

'That's the point, I think. You don't give anyone the chance.'

'Ah, that is most perceptive—at least I think it is.'

'Well, you don't need to try to work it through, because this is where I live. You've got to make it up four flights of stairs—there are seventy-five of them, actually. And please do try to be quiet about it. I have neighbours, and I don't want to wake them up.'

'It wouldn't do for them to know that you came home after dawn, and with a man at that!' he grinned.

'No, that's not what bothers me. It's that they work normal hours and I don't, so I always try to be considerate of them.' Which wasn't strictly true, she decided, unlocking the street door. She didn't want them hearing a great commotion on the stairs, coming to their doors to find her with the highly recognisable Jonathan Worth trailing in her wake.

But the stairs were deeply carpeted, muffling their steps, and Jonathan said nothing until Livia had let them into her own apartment. Then he leaned against the door, expelling a large breath.

'That's quite a price to pay for a cup of coffee!'

'But you're getting bacon and eggs, too, so you'll have the strength to get back down.'

'Actually I only counted seventy-three,' he said.

'You must have blacked out for a second. Believe me, there are seventy-five. I count them every time I carry up groceries. Why don't you go into the living room while I start the coffee?'

'You aren't going to change into something a bit more comfortable first?' he asked with a wicked glint in his eyes.

'Certainly not. That's not why you're here.' He had, to say the least, a certain reputation—something she'd momentarily forgotten when she invited him for breakfast. The trick now was to be quite cool and composed and very much in control of the situation.

'You needn't worry, love. And you needn't look so steely and Queen Victoria-ish. Having worked out so carefully just how long it is since I've had any sleep to speak of, you ought to know that there's nothing to worry about.' He gave her his wicked grin and then his face was suddenly serious as he looked down at her with thoughtful eyes. 'That wouldn't be the case, of course, under more normal circumstances. You're very lovely.'

His eyes lingered, studying her face, making her feel just the least bit breathless. He was attractive in a strange sort of way—physically attractive, in spite of his almost haggard face. More than that, Livia found appealing the endless contradictions, the mercurial changes in mood. But standing in her cramped hallway, feeling absurdly small in his presence, was not the best idea in the world. If she didn't take control right now, something foolish and possibly destructive was about to happen; she didn't believe for a minute what he'd said about lack of sleep. Almost reluctantly she decided that she'd better take control.

'You never stop trying, do you? I should think, at least once, it would be nice to feel that you didn't have to live up to your publicity.' She patted his arm kindly, almost as she might have patted Perry's. 'Besides, you've already scored one conquest this night, with Honey.'

'Only a potential one,' he disagreed, mocking himself.

'You'd have managed, if you hadn't become encumbered with me. Now do stop bothering me, so I can get us some breakfast. As it happens, I haven't had anything to eat in the last day, except for a can of soup. I'm hungry, even if you're not.' With that, she gave him a gentle shove towards the living room door, thinking, as she did so, how totally strange this whole business was. She really shouldn't be ordering Jonathan Worth around with quite such authority.

But he did as she directed, something about his back suggesting a contrite schoolboy. It was dazzling, she thought, staring after him, how he could suggest so much without a word.

She went into the kitchen to start the coffee and to rummage through the refrigerator for the bacon and eggs she had promised. Beyond, in the living room, she could hear him moving slowly around, as though he were examining her things. After a moment, he called out to her.

'To set the record straight, I think I ought to point out that I did not *become* encumbered with you. I chose to encumber myself with you, quite deliberately—with a little planned co-operation from Dickon.'

There seemed to be no reason not to let that one pass, so she did, concentrating on prying bacon loose from the pound.

'Didn't you hear me?' he demanded from the living room.

'Yes, I heard you.' She continued with the bacon.

'Well,' he prompted, appearing in the doorway,

'aren't you going to express some appreciation? Worship at the shrine just a bit?'

Livia dropped the bacon into the pan and lit the gas, taking care to adjust the flame properly, before turning to look at him. 'Let me get this straight,' she said very deliberately. 'I'm supposed to be grateful because you made a perfect ass of yourself with Honey Pressman for most of the evening, and then dropped her—at the last possible moment—so that I could take you home and make you breakfast.'

Jonathan smiled a little selfconsciously. 'Put quite that way it doesn't sound as good.'

'No, it doesn't. Besides,' she continued, cracking eggs with a certain viciousness, 'yesterday you told me not to worship at the shrine.'

'Oh, I talk a lot of rubbish—you know that.'

'Yes,' she agreed absently, turning bacon with a fork. 'But I don't think you were, then. I've always heard people say, "Begin as you mean to go on," and I always thought it was a silly thing to say, because how could one know how one meant to go on, until after one had begun. But I think I've found the one time in my life when I can apply that principle. Do you like your bacon rare or well done?'

'I've never thought of bacon in quite those terms,' he said with some amusement. 'I like it burned to a crisp, actually. But please don't let the bacon divert you from what I hope will be a fascinating statement.

'Where was I?' she asked.

'Beginning where you meant to go on.'

'All right, then. I do not intend to treat you like some sort of god. I shall not fall at your feet and worship. I'm well over that stage, thanks to your behaviour in the past few hours. You're a better actor than I—and don't you dare deny it,' she added with some heat, seeing the protest forming. 'Of course you are, and all that talk about tearing it out of yourself, and supposing that I can do it with no effort at all, is foolish. So, I'll grant that you're a better actor, but not that you're a better person. And if you think I ought to be grateful because you ditched Honey to bring me home—well, that's your problem, not mine. I do not intend to spend the next few months being grateful every time you attempt to throw me a personal crumb.'

'I see.' For a moment Livia thought he was truly angry. 'You're going to take the approach that you're impervious to my manifest charms.' The slight glint in his eyes, at the end, reassured her.

'Oh, you have a certain charm,' she allowed. 'But I think that you appeal more to people like Honey.' She swept by him to set the table, totally abandoning the bacon. He was carefully lifting it out of the pan when she returned to the kitchen.

'You don't mind, do you?' he asked. 'I began to get the feeling that your idea of crisp and mine are not precisely the same.'

Livia felt her resolution failing, because he was suddenly quite human, quite nice about the bacon and—she was forced to admit—quite charming. She finished cooking in silence, while Jonathan leaned against the door frame, watching her. She was grateful that he didn't try to provoke her again. Cooking absorbed enough of her thinking, without having to engage in verbal sparring—particularly with Jonathan Worth, who was obviously a master at it.

He's studying me, she decided, trying to see where he can drive the next wedge. He would seduce her, if given a chance. Not physically, perhaps, although a small corner of her mind was not convinced of that. But he could also seduce her emotionally, or spiritually. He claimed not to want her as a worshipper, and yet he was doing his best to make her one. She was filled with righteous indignation which lasted only until the food was on the table, and she sat down.

She could see the energy draining out of him, as he took the chair opposite hers. She realised with a pang precisely how much effort he had been putting into simply remaining upright.

'Why do you try so hard?' She sounded almost motherly in her concern.

'I haven't the slightest idea.' Jonathan sipped his coffee before absently lighting a cigarette, leaving the food untouched. 'If I knew that I wouldn't do it, would I?' He smiled crookedly and then rubbed his forehead with his free hand.

'Is it because people expect it of you?'

'No. It's come to be what people expect of me, so I suppose there are times when that's why I continue on. But I was doing it long before anyone had any expectations at all.' He paused for a moment, studying the rim of his cup. 'I suppose it's what I expect of myself, but that's not much of an answer, is it? And it gets worse, as the years pass. Perhaps, if I hadn't made quite such a name for myself, it wouldn't be so bad. Because you're right—a lot of it is because people expect it of me. I'm supposed to be the life of the party. I'm supposed to be outrageous and tell marvellous stories—not that I mind so much, because I do have a passion for marvellous stories. But it's the expectation people have. I don't know why I have to satisfy it, but I do. You were quite right about one other thing, you know.'

'What's that?'

'It *was* tea I was drinking tonight.'

'I didn't think you heard that,' Livia confessed.

'Not much, but I did get the very beginning.' He

stubbed out the cigarette in his saucer and picked up a piece of bacon. 'Do you realise what I do? People think I'm this great drinker—which I was, of course, a long time ago. But I realised that I wasn't going to be able to keep the act together, if I continued, so I stopped. But I couldn't let them know that, could I? So I bring along my own bottle, and make a great scene about how this is mine, and no one else is to touch it. And then I drink weak tea all evening. That is insane, isn't it?'

'A bit.'

'Not many people know that,' he added, digging into his breakfast with a certain enthusiasm. 'Apparently I trust you, or I wouldn't have told you. But I'd rather that it didn't become general knowledge, if you don't mind.'

'I'm not going to tell tales,' she said, exasperation mixed with pity, and then watched while he finished the food and drained his cup. 'Would you like anything more?'

He shook his head, began to reach for another cigarette and then appeared to think better of it. 'Look, I'm sure you're about to feel that I'm making improper advances, but I absolutely cannot go back to that hotel room now. Would you mind awfully if I just took your couch for a few hours?' Before she could start an answer, he hurried on. 'I promise you, I haven't got even one ulterior motive in my head. In fact, I haven't got much of anything in my head, escept an overwhelming desire to get some sleep. You'll be quite safe.'

There were quite a few things she might have liked to say to him, all of them either tart or provoking. But he looked too tired to handle anything at all. 'I'll get a pillow and a blanket.'

When she came back, he was already stretched out

on the couch, hands behind his head, staring up at the ceiling. 'You've got an interesting ceiling here,' he started, and Livia could feel the effort, as he tried to summon energy for one last attempt at doing what was expected.

She knelt down on the floor beside him and touched his lips lightly with her fingers. 'Don't try. Don't bother to try.' And then she slipped the pillow under his head and watched him turn gratefully into it. She rose silently and carefully spread the blanket over him, thinking that perhaps he was already, instantly, off to sleep. But he wasn't.

Without opening his eyes, he smiled briefly. 'You're a grand girl, Livia. And I can't think why anyone calls you Livy. It doesn't suit you in the least, you know.'

'I know,' she agreed in a whisper, and then watched while his breathing grew deep and even, studying a face which suddenly looked completely empty. Fragile was what Dickon had called him, and Livia had to agree. But she wondered why he should look most fragile when there was no emotion at all in his face.

CHAPTER THREE

LIVIA set her alarm for six, undressed, and climbed into bed. She began to slip off to sleep, surrounded in her mind by crowds of laughing people. Then, unexpectedly, Jonathan Worth appeared, looming above the rest, and she snapped awake for the moment it took for him to disappear. He came around quite a few times, until she began to wonder if she'd ever be free of him. But he finally receded and she slept deeply, with no dreams at all.

The insistent buzzing of the alarm clock finally intruded and she switched it off, taking a quick look out the window as she did so. It was raining, which meant a wet and considerably less than inspiring walk to the theatre. Life seemed depressingly flat—a thought she hated to acknowledge because it led straight back to Jonathan Worth.

She padded down the hallway to the kitchen, supposing it would be soup again tonight. When she pulled on the light she saw the frying pan, left over from breakfast, still on the stove. She sighed, realising that she would have to clear away the dishes from the table in the living room. She'd have the dubious consolation of scraping Jonathan Worth's cigarette butt from his saucer.

She started into the living room to begin the job, and then stopped dead in the doorway. Even though the light was dim—just a yellow slant from the kitchen and dull grey from the bay window—it was obvious that her guest was still with her. Everything in the room was shades of grey, blurring off to black, but there was no mistaking the form under the blanket.

She retreated for a moment, before curiosity won and she stole in to have a look. Jonathan's face was still all planes and angles, although somewhat smudged in the dusk. His nose was rather hawkish, she decided, although that seemed a silly analogy. Hawks didn't have noses. Still, she didn't know how else to describe a nose which was high-bridged, narrow, and just a trifle arrogant. His cheekbones were quite pronounced, which seemed to explain why his face had such a taut, stretched look to it—that and his chin, which had a decided angularity of its own. While he missed, somehow, being conventionally handsome, he succeeded in being something infinitely more appealing and interesting. But, she told herself impatiently, this preoccupation was pointless. It was time to get to the theatre.

When she went into her dressing room, she found Dickon carefully and precisely rearranging her make-up stuff. Dickon abhorred clutter, making Livia wonder how he came to be so wrapped up in the theatre. Theatres were dirty, messy places at best.

'Oh, hello, Livy,' he began, as though completely surprised to see her in her own dressing room.

Livy! she thought with exasperation. Jonathan was right—it really didn't suit her at all.

'How are you?' Dickon asked with significance. Dickon had quite a knack for significance, Livia decided, wondering why she'd never noticed it before.

'Well, I'm fine, Dickon. Is there any reason why I shouldn't be?' There was a slight edge to her voice, because Dickon obviously felt there was a reason why she shouldn't or wouldn't be fine. The reason almost certainly had something to do with Jonathan.

'Livy,' he said with some reproach, avoiding her eyes, 'you left last night with Jon, and I know him far better than you.'

'Well, of course you do, Dickon,' she said evenly, not willing to make it any easier for him. 'But I don't see what that has to do with how I am. Besides, we left this morning, not last night.'

'Livy, I want to know if he—well, if he upset you in any way.'

'You mean, did he rape and pillage me? Oh, Dickon, don't look so terribly unamused!' His eyes, looking slightly hangdog, met hers in the mirror. 'He walked me home, came in, and I gave him breakfast. He was a perfect gentleman.' That much, at least, was true. Somehow Livia thought it might be better not to mention that he was still asleep on her couch.

'I tried to reach him all afternoon at the hotel, but they said that he hadn't come in.'

'Well, don't look at me,' Livia exclaimed, doing one of her better jobs of acting, she thought. 'I can't help it if he doesn't go back to his hotel.' That much, too, was true. She couldn't help it, if he wanted to sleep on her couch and hadn't wakened up yet.

Dickon finally smiled, his careful, precise and guarded smile. 'I'm sorry, Livy. But I know him awfully well, you see. He can run through girls like you with no trouble at all.'

'At twenty-nine, I'm hardly a girl,' she said wryly. 'And I think you might find that I have a bit more backbone than you give me credit for. But I didn't need it, this morning. Perhaps Jonathan doesn't deserve the reputation you think he has.'

'Or perhaps he was just too tired.'

'Or perhaps he went back to Honey. Now do get out, Dickon. I've been asleep all day and I'd like to spend just a little time getting into Candida, before the show starts.'

'All right.' He stood up heavily—still ponderous,

Livia noted. 'But you can't blame me for worrying, Livy.'

'I certainly can!' she exclaimed, with more sharpness than she had intended. And then, seeing his stricken look, she added, 'But I'm not going to hold it against you.' She patted his cheek absently, as he brushed by her in the tiny room. Then she sat down in front of the mirror, waiting for Candida—dear calm Candida—to arrive on the scene and make sense out of her conflicting emotions.

Candida's calm was still with her after the performance, that and a fine sense of emptiness. Just as well, she told herself ruefully, walking home in the rain. She didn't really want to go back to an empty apartment right now. Much as she hated to admit it, she wanted to see Jonathan again. Candida's calm and her own supply of emptiness seemed the best way to handle her feelings.

When she let herself in the apartment, a little breathless from the climb, she stopped dead—that seemed to be a habit she was acquiring. The kitchen light was on, as she had left it, and through the door she could see the dishes stacked neatly in the drainer. But there was more to it than that. One light burned dimly in the living room and the stereo was playing quite softly. Livia stood motionless, one hand lightly touching the doorknob, not quite wanting to believe.

'And how was *Candida* tonight?' the familiar voice called from the living room. She heard the creaking of the rocking chair and footsteps on the bare floor. Then Jonathan appeared in the doorway—filling it, actually.

'I thought you'd be gone by now,' she said more calmly than she felt, pulling the door closed behind her.

'I haven't been up so awfully long. I hope you don't mind that I've been making myself at home.'

She shook her head. 'You did the dishes.' There was a certain wonder in her voice.

'That's not so extraordinary, is it?'

'No. It would have been a bit sticky, wouldn't it, if I'd brought someone home with me?'

'I thought of that, but I somehow thought you wouldn't, tonight.' He flashed her his engaging grin.

'I did think you'd be long gone,' she pointed out with some heat.

'I know,' he agreed mildly. 'You told me that. I don't assume that you've come home alone tonight because of me, you know. Perhaps it was intuition. I also thought you'd be hungry. I expect you forgot to eat before the show.'

Livia nodded.

'It was kind of you to leave me in peace. You must have been very quiet about it, because I don't sleep very soundly as a general rule. And I could tell that you hadn't got yourself anything to eat here. So I went out and explored your neighbourhood. Look, why don't you take off your coat and stay a while?'

She laughed out loud at that. 'You do know how to take the high ground, don't you?'

'I'm not quite sure what that means.' He waited while she took off her coat. 'I should think you'd want to sit down,' he prompted, and she felt a bit like a child, following him obediently into her own living room. 'At any rate, I explored your neighbourhood——' he obviously wanted to tell his story—was quite smug about it, actually—'and found myself a little store where I could buy a razor.' He rubbed a freshly shaved cheek appreciatively. 'Your neighbourhood doesn't seem to have a haberdashers, so I couldn't do anything about a crumpled shirt.'

'You ought to have used my iron,' Livia put in, and he grinned.

'Well, that seemed a bit personal, somehow. Besides, I didn't know where it was. But I did find a very nice little deli, about two blocks from here. You probably know it.'

She nodded tolerantly, dropping into the chair on the far side of the empty fireplace.

'It appears to be a combination of Greek and Italian, and they have quite an impressive spread of stuff. Since I assumed that you hadn't eaten, and knew I hadn't, I thought it might be most logical to pick something up, so we could make a meal. Unless, of course, you'd like to go out.'

'Lord, no!' She could imagine the circus they might generate, if anyone recognised him in a public place. Besides, her feet hurt, and she didn't relish the idea of tramping back down the seventy-five steps. With that thought in mind, she kicked off her shoes and stretched her feet.

'You do look tired. Why do you try so hard?' Jonathan was mocking her with her own words to him. But, before she could rise to the bait, he continued. 'I'm sorry. I'm trying to be quite normal, right now, so as not to provoke you in the least. I will try to keep the joking to a minimum, but you must realise that I can't always contain myself.'

'Oh, I'm fully aware of that.'

'At any rate, I found clean knives and forks and plates, and I hope I've got enough food to satisfy us.' He started towards the kitchen. 'I also found a little wine shop, so you have your choice of red or white.'

'You're going to stick with tea, I presume?'

'No. I've made coffee. You're welcome to that, if you like. I'll tell you what we have.' He disappeared into the kitchen, and she heard the refrigerator door open. 'There's ham or chicken, or liverwurst, and Greek salad or coleslaw, potato salad, and some bagels with cream cheese, and some rather extraordinary Greek pastries. I decided against the stuffed vine leaves. I thought you might find them a bit suggestive.'

'I can't imagine why,' Livia said mildly.

'They rather smack of a Roman orgy, don't you think? Or perhaps a Grecian one.' He reappeared, carrying an assortment of paper containers. 'It won't be very nicely served—I hope you don't mind.'

'I don't.'

'Now, do you want red wine or white? I found a wine glass—several, in fact, but I only needed one.'

'Red, I think. Red is nice and fuzzy, if it's cheap enough.'

'I expect this is. It's got a screw cap.' Jonathan came back with the wine bottle and the coffee pot. 'There, I think that's it.' He looked thoughtfully down at the table. 'Am I trying too dreadfully hard?'

'I'd say so.' Livia got up, barefoot, to take the chair he was holding out for her. 'But right now I'm prepared to accept it.'

'Yes. You'll be much restored after you've eaten.' He gave her a grin. 'Then you can begin to do your best to tear me to shreds!'

'I haven't been like that, have I?' she asked with innocence, and began opening containers.

'No, but you're perilously close to it, I think. Quite unjustified, because I'm only trying to be nice. Which is not something I do very often.'

'I'm sure of that.' She served herself, passing things on to him as she finished with them.

'I like that dress,' he observed, after they had begun to eat. 'You wore it last night, and I meant to mention it.'

'Oh lord!' she exclaimed, putting down her fork. 'No wonder Dickon gave me such a reproachful look!'

'And when did you see him?' Jonathan asked idly.

'He was waiting for me at the theatre. He gave me a bit of a lecture—about you.' Briefly, she described the exchange, managing mouthfuls of food as she did so.

'Good thing you didn't bring him home,' Jonathan observed as she finished. 'After you'd gone and lied, or at least stretched the truth to the breaking point. Most compromising. Poor old Dickon couldn't handle that.' He poured her more wine, cleaned his plate and then leaned back to light a cigarette.

He did look better, Livia decided. Not that any of the planes and angles had disappeared, but there was a bit more colour to his face, and the whole line of his body suggested greater ease. She felt better, too— much restored, to use Jonathan's words. She pushed her plate away and sipped at her wine.

'So you had to tell Dickon that I hadn't raped and pillaged you,' said Jonathan, with a smile. 'I'd have liked to see his face when you made that particular comment. You do have an ability to really fire away, haven't you? Now, I expect, it's my turn to be on the receiving end.'

'Oh, I don't feel like firing away at you, Jonathan. Do you know, I almost always think of you as Jonathan Worth—all one word. It seems a bit strange to call you only Jonathan, and leave the rest of it off.'

'You haven't before—called me Jonathan. You haven't called me anything at all, in fact. Anyway, Jonathan Worth is some sort of an institution. I don't know much about him. Perhaps you're beginning to see me as something other than an institution.' He smiled. 'That would be nice.'

'Well, it is a little difficult to view as an institution someone who does one's dishes and brings home supper.'

'I hoped it would be. There's something about you,

Livia, although I'm not sure just what it is.' He stubbed out his cigarette and immediately lit another. 'I've been trying to figure it out, the past couple of hours. You're not after me, for one thing, and that's a bit of a change. And you're not the most attractive girl in the world, although you are quite lovely. You have a certain grace, or composure—I'm not quite sure what it is. But it's quite striking; one notices it immediately. You were quite dazzling at the party last night, because you were so different from anyone else there. And I'm putting this rather badly, I'm afraid, because what you look like really has nothing to do with how I feel about you.' He frowned and looked away, and Livia could tell that he was having a difficult time.

'There's something very warm about you, or very steadying. I'm quite drawn to you. In fact, I want you rather badly.' And before Livia could say anything at all—not that she had any idea what to say—he laughed. 'Now I've made a complete ass of myself! Do forgive me. But I thought it important that you understand my sudden reformation. Not that I understand it awfully well myself. You see, it was quite nice to do something for you while you were at the theatre. I had quite the feeling of purpose— something I don't usually have, except about my work. I thought that if I behaved myself, you might view me with some approval.'

He stood up abruptly. 'Now I think I'd better go, before I make a complete fool of myself and make things any worse than they are now.'

'But you haven't,' she protested. He seemed poised for flight, and she didn't want him to leave until she'd made herself clear. So she got up and took his free hand with both of hers. 'You've been very flattering, and I don't mind it a bit.'

'I didn't intend to be flattering,' he said impatiently. 'I was making an attempt to be about as real as I think I'm capable of being.'

'You didn't let me finish,' she reproved, and smiled up at him. 'I was going to say that I liked what you had to say. I think I'm quite drawn to you, too.'

'Livia.' It was almost a question, but not quite. He studied her face for a moment and then, suddenly, his arms were around her and his lips touching hers—tentatively, just at first, and then with increasing confidence. Livia's arms came up to hold him closely, partly wanting, irrationally, to comfort him, and partly wanting, without thought, to be as near to him as possible. His lips were on her throat, and hers against his temple, and she felt both a passion and a tenderness quite unlike anything she'd ever felt before. It was absolutely glorious and quite right—she knew that without giving it a thought.

'Do you want to stay?' she heard herself whisper, and felt his sigh.

'Yes.' His lips returned to hers, searching deeply, before he suddenly broke away, placing his hands firmly on her shoulders. 'But I'm not going to.' He looked both torn and puzzled. 'I'm not going to spoil this one, Livia,' he said quietly, and then continued with greater passion, but a different sort of passion. 'I've got to leave in the morning, and I will not let this be just one in a succession of different nights. I want some substance—can you understand that?'

She nodded and then smiled briefly. 'It will have substance.' She wanted very badly for him to stay. She wanted to hold him without any constraints at all, to share everything with him.

'No, Livia. I've had too many single nights. I will not have another one, not with you. I know myself too well.' He shrugged. 'Let me have my noble gesture, please?'

She nodded, biting her lower lip, because it wasn't what she wanted, not in the least. But she could understand that what he wanted had far more meaning.

With one hand he traced the line of her face, from her forehead to her chin. 'I'll come back in the spring,' he promised, 'and then we can begin as we mean to go on.' He smiled crookedly, kissed her once again, but briefly, this time. Then, without another word, he left her and walked out of the room.

Livia stood motionless, hearing the sound of the door as it opened and closed behind him, and then the sound of his footsteps growing fainter on the stairs, until she couldn't hear them at all.

CHAPTER FOUR

JONATHAN was gone, and there seemed no hope of
contact with him until he returned in the spring. An
awkward business, Livia thought grimly—getting
quite so involved so quickly, and then having the
object of one's involvement dash off to the other side
of the world. It left too many loose ends: things she
would have liked to have settled with Jonathan. And
obviously, none of them were going to be settled while
he was gone. Jonathan—she knew this with sure
conviction—was not the sort to write. It wasn't his
style to try to settle anything on a bloodless piece of
paper.

There was nothing to do, she decided with as much
composure as possible, but to get herself through the
months until his return. There was the run of *Candida*
to finish, before the Christmas break. Then the
company would pull out its old production of *Julius
Caesar* to run until the first week in March.
Immediately after that, Jonathan would arrive, and
rehearsals on Dickon's new play could begin. With
that, Livia had to be content.

It developed, however, that she had been wrong
about one thing. Jonathan might not be the sort to
settle things by mail, but he did write. The much
battered airmail envelope was waiting for her at the
end of a particularly cold and lonely day of dull
routine.

She tore it open with unsteady fingers and saw his
bold and angular handwriting—larger than life, she
realised, like the man himself.

'Livia——

'Did you really tell Dickon that I hadn't raped and pillaged you? I rather like that line—you have a good ear for what sounds well. I've been mulling it over in my mind. Here in this wretched jungle, it seems to create one of the bright points of my day. Perhaps it's not so much the line (although I *do* like it) as the fact that I didn't rape and pillage you. That gives me a certain satisfaction—I can't think why.

'You may be reading about me soon, because some silly hack was here, looking to retell the same old story. He talked with me and wasn't pleased, because I was disappointingly flat—it isn't easy to be anything else in a bloody jungle. Then he dug up what he could find from the others in the cast and crew. Some of them were anxious to oblige. I'm afraid that I won't come off as a paragon of all possible virtues, and I hope you'll disregard at least the majority of what is written.

'They make a great point of what I'm earning for this thing, but I ought to have asked for more. The climate and the accommodations are less than acceptable—to say the least. Too hot—I lean my head against an ice cube (when I can get my hands on one) and wish I were in Boston, where it must be cold by now.

'At least, unlike the rest, I won't be here the full time. Still, Christmas in this hole will seem a bit bizarre.

'I'm running on to no point, which isn't like me— at least not on paper. I don't write letters, you know, which just shows how much this jungle—and you, I suppose—have done to me.

'When you read the article, please don't begin to doubt my reformation. The only problem is, and

I'm afraid you'll just have to accept it, that it appears to begin and end with you. Perhaps you can understand what that really means.

'Jonathan'

It wasn't the most conventional of love letters; Livia wasn't sure if she ought to think of it as one at all. But it *was* Jonathan, a little contact with him, something to carry her through the long months to come.

It also helped when Maureen rushed up one day to share the offending magazine article.

'You've got to hear this!' she announced, settling herself on the couch and proceeding to read it aloud with great relish.

The title was 'Paying the Piper', and the article went on at some length about Jonathan's labours in the jungle, the fact that he was doing a limited role for a lot of money. The film role, he explained, was allowing him to justify the time and loss of income a new play in Boston would absorb. At considerably greater length, the story went on to rehash his legendary exploits—the rumoured wild nights and endless women. Now, according to the writer, Jonathan Worth was finding fresh possibilities in a rain forest, and looking much the worse for wear because of them.

Having got that far, Maureen looked up to be sure that Livia was paying the proper attention. 'Now,' she cautioned seriously, 'You've got to listen carefully, because *you* get mentioned, and I expect you've never been in a national magazine before.'

She went back to the page and hunted for the proper lines. 'It says, 'He's paying the piper, it would appear, not only for a play in Boston, but for past and present excesses. It remains to be seen if this man of extremes will moderate his pace, when he begins his new work in Boston. Friends doubt it; his new leading lady, Livia Paige, is reported to be a fresh and attractive new face. And when has Jonathan Worth ever been able to resist one of those?" You see, Livy?' Maureen demanded, not missing a beat. 'You're a fresh and attractive new face—and millions of people are going to read it!'

'And promptly forget all about it,' Livia observed dryly. 'And I'm not sure I like being described as nothing more than the next in a long series of conquests.'

'But it gets you in the news,' Maureen said sagely. 'What is it they say? It doesn't matter what they print, as long as they get your name right.'

'That's never been my feeling,' Livia said shortly, and wished Maureen would stop. Something quite private and important was happening, or was about to happen, between her and Jonathan. She didn't like to see her name and his spread around in magazines, and she was tired of Maureen's casual enthusiasm—no matter how well-meaning it was intended to be.

It was a relief to be done with *Candida* and to be able to escape to Vermont and a family whose approach was very different. Everyone was pleased for her, because she had managed to get a good part in a good play, and the chance to appear with someone really important. But they weren't trying to create a romance, and they didn't speculate endlessly about unknown possibilities.

It was a large and happy group. Livia was an only child, but her father's two brothers and their families lived nearby, and the relatives lived very much in each other's pockets. Livia, older than her cousins, was the only member of the family to have moved away. That in itself was something of a novelty, and having her home was even more of one. She served as a drawing card, bringing the others to her parents' house.

Most evenings, various members of the family gathered, usually around the dining room table, where they played games or talked or—most frequently—did both at the same time. Most of these evenings tended to go on into the small hours of the morning. (Jonathan would feel right at home, Livia told herself with a secret smile.)

So, when the telephone rang at a quarter past two on one of those late evenings, it didn't wake a sleeping house. But everyone stopped talking and looked around, trying to see who wasn't there, who might have been involved in an accident. In the ordered world of Livia's family, calls at this hour were always bad news. The phone rang a second time and, because she had an almost certain conviction about the call, Livia got up to answer it.

An operator's voice, sounding distant, said, 'Miss Olivia Paige, please.'

'Speaking,' she answered automatically. 'But it's Livia——' Which didn't seem to matter, because she could hear the operator already speaking in the opposite direction.

'I have your party on the line.'

And then, very faintly and with considerable static, so that she was grateful for the still expectant hush around the dining room table two rooms away, she heard Jonathan's voice. 'Livia, is that you? It's Jonathan,' he added unnecessarily.

'Yes, I know,' she answered normally.

'You'll have to speak up.'

'Yes, it's Livia!' she shouted, trying to make each word distinct. Behind her she could feel those seated at the table leaning forward, collectively curious. 'Wait a minute, please.' And then, to the assembled family, she called, 'It's a business call for me. No one got hurt.' And, while that might relieve the worry in the group, it did nothing for the curiosity factor.

'Have I got you in front of a group of people?' Jonathan asked, with some perception, Livia thought, given the poor connection.

'That's right!' she yelled.

'Well then, I'll have to say things properly, so you can give noncommittal answers, won't I?'

'That's right!' she yelled again, feeling more than a little silly. 'Why are you calling?' That seemed reasonably noncommittal.

'I'm not really sure, to tell the truth. But I went to so much work to get you, in the first place, that I decided I might as well talk to you. You see, I've been calling Boston for the past week, and getting no answer. So I decided that you must have gone away for the holidays. And I decided that you're the sort of girl to go home for the holidays—making the assumption that you have a home, which is something not everyone has, you know.' Jonathan, she realised, viewed a foreign telephone call as no different from a face-to-face conversation. He wasn't going to worry about the rates, not when he had a good story to tell. 'So I called my agent in New York, and asked him to find out where you lived—at least the town. And then I had to call him back, because he couldn't get through to me, for some unknown reason. I'd have thought that the capabilities of the New York telephone system would be greater than those of the one out here. However, I found out where you live, or where your parents live, but I didn't know your father's first name. So I've been calling every Paige in whatever town it is that you live—the minor details begin to escape me by now. None of the other Paiges answered—there are only three of them, actually, including you—and the poor operator has been in despair. What time is it there?' he asked in an abrupt shift.

'A little after two.'

'Morning or afternoon?'

'Morning.'

'Oh. Good thing that none of the other Paiges were home, isn't it?'

'That's because they're all here.'

'Really?' Even though the connection was faint and filled with interference, Livia could hear the arrested interest in his voice. 'At this hour of the night, too. Sounds as though I ought to fit right in.' It was so exactly what Livia had been thinking, earlier, that she was left with nothing suitable to say. 'Are you still there?' Jonathan demanded.

'Yes.'

'I thought I'd lost you. Would I fit right in?'

'I expect so.'

'God knows, anything would be better than being here—not that I mean to slight you or your family. But this is a wretched place. There are leeches.'

'There are what?' she shouted.

'Leeches. You know—those little devils that stick to you and try to suck out the blood. We've been filming in a bloody swamp, and they attach themselves whenever it suits their fancy. We have to burn them off.'

'I'm sorry,' Livia said, inadequately, acutely aware of the listeners in the dining room.

'Yes, you ought to be. And I've got to be here longer than I thought. Things are moving slowly, which isn't surprising, given leeches and various and sundry other obstacles. It's a frightful mess, not helped a bit by the fact that they don't know exactly what they're doing.'

'I'm sorry,' Livia shouted again, and wished that she could say something more personal. But she'd told her family that it was a business call, and she was locked into sounding like one end of a business call.

'I shall be back in time for rehearsals, though. You needn't worry about that.'

'I wasn't.'

'No? Then perhaps you were worrying about me?' he asked with a touch of humour.

'Perhaps. Yes.'

'You do manage to be frightfully noncommittal, don't you? I gather, then, that you are worrying about me?'

'Yes.' Again!

'I suppose that I've got to think up a lot of nice things for you to say, and then say them for you.'

'That's right.'

'Well, then, that gives me quite a bit of latitude, doesn't it? And you'd better say yes to everything I say, because my morale needs a bit of a boost, I can tell you that. I'm actually quite lonely, Livia. This is not what you might call a compatible group.'

'I'm sorry.' And she was, sincerely, although there didn't seem any way to convey more feeling.

'So—now I shall play on your sympathies, and you'd better say yes to everything. Do you love me?'

Outrageous, she thought—he was being totally outrageous. 'Yes,' she shouted. 'At the moment.'

'And do you miss me extravagantly?'

'Yes.'

'And will you marry me, as soon as I get out of this damned hole and back to Boston?'

'Don't talk rubbish!' she shouted, coming completely out of character.

'Ah, that struck a chord, didn't it? It's also going to be difficult to explain to the family. What are you going to tell them, anyway?' There was a pause, while she waited helplessly. 'Of course, you can't say, can you?'

'No.'

'Some sort of nonsense, and I expect you'll carry it off quite well, too.' Even though Jonathan, too, was yelling, she could hear the sudden softening in his voice. 'Livia, I wish I could see you.'

'I do, too.'

There was a moment's pause at his end. 'A phone call doesn't help as much as I hoped it might.'

'I am sorry.' That seemed to be as close as she could come to letting him know how she felt.

'That's good to know. I'll hang on to that.'

'Yes, you should. Are you well?'

'I suppose so. Lost a bit of weight, I expect. One really doesn't feel like eating in all this heat. I——' He faltered briefly and then resumed, voice confident again. 'Livia, you really ought to tell your family that I was calling from a bloody rain forest to ask you to marry me.'

'I think not,' she said firmly.

'Very well, then, I'll have to tell them myself. In the natural course of events, I'll meet them, and I'll say, "Do you remember that strange call Livia got back at Christmas time? The one where she said nothing but yes and no? Well, she didn't want to tell you, but I was asking her to marry me." That ought to impress them, don't you think? I expect you haven't been so monosyllabic since you were an infant. They must all be wondering what's gotten into you, to render you nearly speechless.'

'I expect it's been quite unpleasant,' she began, seized with a sudden inspiration as to how to get her point across. 'I know you'll feel differently when you get out of there.'

'Nicely put, Livia, but you're wrong. Dead wrong, in fact. They gave us three days off, because of the holidays, although I can't imagine why. There's nowhere to go around here, and three days isn't enough time to go anywhere that's better. But tracking you down has been a welcome diversion—consumed a fair bit of time.'

'I think that's the whole point!' she shouted.

'I know what you're thinking,' said Jonathan, 'that I'm lonely and not having the best of times, so I've gone all maudlin and sentimental.'

'I think so.'

'Well, I haven't. Livia? Couldn't you say something? Nothing too revealing, but something? I rather need things to hang on to, at this point.'

'All right!' she yelled, softening, because she could hear the genuine appeal in his voice. 'It will be good——' Good what? Good how? What was she going to say, with her family hanging avidly on her every word?

'Why don't you leave it at that, Livia? I can feel you trying to frame a suitably noncommittal qualifying phrase. It will be good, Livia, I promise you that. And don't forget to tell me what your inventive little mind comes up with, to explain all this to your family. I can't wait to hear.'

'All right,' she promised.

'I guess it's rather pointless to prolong this. Merry Christmas, Livia.'

'And to you.'

'Not possible, in this hole—a contradiction in terms. I'll see you before too long.' And then, quite abruptly, before she could say anything else, he had hung up. She stared blankly at the phone for a moment or two and then replaced the receiver.

'Who was that?' her uncle demanded as she came back into the dining room.

'Jonathan Worth,' she answered, feeling a bit bemused, and deciding that attitude might be the best way to play things.

'Are you sure?' It was one of her cousins, sounding sceptical.

'Well, of course I'm sure. I have met him, you know. Anyway, there's no danger of being unsure where Jonathan Worth is concerned.'

'Why was he calling you?'

'I really don't know.' Livia wrinkled her brow. This ought to look as puzzling to her as to the others. 'He's off in Malaya, making a movie—in a wretched jungle, he called it. He said he wanted to talk about the play.'

'Did he?'

'To a certain extent. He had some new ideas on how it could be improved.' Unworthy, Livia thought briefly—lying to your family. 'But I think that he mostly wanted to complain about living conditions.'

'Then why did he pick you'

'That I can't tell you. I shouldn't have thought he knew me well enough to go to the bother.'

'*You* didn't have much to say,' her father pointed out, knowing her well enough to realise what was out of character.

'No one has much to say when Jonathan Worth is talking. Besides, it was his nickel, and I didn't think I ought to be using it up. A very strange call.'

'Perhaps he's sweet on you, Livy,' suggested Karen, the youngest of the cousins.

'I doubt it. At least, he didn't seem to be when he was in Boston. He made a frightful play for Honey Pressman—she's the sexy blonde in the company.'

'Well, perhaps he's going to get sweet on you, and this was the opening round.' Karen was an incurable romantic.

'I really don't think so,' Livia said reprovingly. 'I'm

really not his type. And he's certainly not mine—much too outrageous and flamboyant for my taste.'

That seemed to settle it for the others, but she noticed her mother's occasional thoughtful glances. She couldn't possibly have heard the conversation, Livia knew. Did it show on her face? she wondered. Could a mother tell when her daughter received a proposal of marriage? Not that it was a serious proposal, Livia told herself hastily. Jonathan was lonely and bored, and had simply needed to make some sort of outrageous gesture. Well, he had done so, but nothing was settled. Their future would still have to wait until he came back.

CHAPTER FIVE

LIVIA returned to Boston and the rehearsals for *Julius Caesar* with a lack of interest she found almost frightening. Coming back to Boston held no special joy—not with Jonathan far away and not expected for several weeks. And *Caesar* seemed, at this point, the flattest and least exciting of projects. Her own role, that of Caesar's wife, was insignificant to the point of boredom, and rehearsals held none of the enthusiasm she had come to expect.

It was obvious that no one in the company was particularly thrilled with *Caesar*. Like Livia (although not for precisely the same reasons, she reminded herself with a secret smile) everyone appeared to be marking time, waiting for Jonathan to return. Given the general lack of enthusiasm, Livia assumed that her own attitude would pass unnoticed, but she found that Perry was more perceptive than the others.

'What's the matter, Livy?' he asked one day during a break. 'You look as though you're right in the middle of the winter of your discontent.'

'I am,' she snapped bitterly and without thought, before deciding that she'd better use a little discretion. It wouldn't do to have anyone—not even Perry—know the extent to which Jonathan, and his absence, dominated her thoughts. 'I can't stand being Caesar's wife,' she added, taking a safer tack.

'It's not the biggest part in the world,' Perry agreed, giving the matter serious thought. 'A bit of a let-down to have this stuck between Candida's part and the chance to be Dickon's woman.'

'It's not that. I don't mind small parts, and some of them are rather fun. But Calpurnia is so dreadfully dull!' Having started off on a diversionary tack, she now found herself quite sincerely feeling the injustice of being Caesar's wife. 'She natters on about dreams and portents, and doesn't want Caesar to go to the Forum—of course, she was right about that, but Caesar didn't believe her, and I shouldn't have, either. I can't stand superstitious women!'

'You're being pretty hard on the old girl,' Perry observed mildly, but studying Livia's face with fresh curiosity.

'Oh, it's not Calpurnia,' she disagreed with a wave of her hand. 'I expect she was a very nice lady, and it can't have been easy, being married to a Caesar—there wouldn't be a lot of security in that position. It's the part I don't like. All that foolishness to say, and then she ends up telling him to call in sick. Have you ever tried to sound convincing, while telling someone to call in sick in Shakespeare's metre?' Livia subsided into brooding depression, stung by the fresh unfairness of it all. It was really too much, to have to handle the lack of Jonathan and the trials of being Calpurnia, all at the same time.

'You'll be a lot happier when Jonathan gets here,' said Perry in an attempt to provide some comfort.

'Why?' Livia demanded, sitting bolt upright and wondering how Perry had managed to see through her smokescreen recital of Calpurnia's faults.

'Because then you'll have a chance to do some really exciting work,' Perry explained patiently. 'The play. Dickon's woman. Remember?'

'Oh, that.' She purposely made her face as expressionless as possible. 'I'd forgotten all about that, for the moment. And I do wish you wouldn't keep calling me Dickon's woman,' She added peevishly.

'I wasn't calling *you* Dickon's woman,' Perry corrected gently. 'I was calling the part that.'

'Well, I wish you wouldn't even call the part Dickon's woman,' Livia amended a little more kindly. 'One of the points of the play is that the woman doesn't belong to anyone. It breaks my concentration when you slap someone else's label on to her. It makes her seem no better than Caesar's wife.'

'Sorry, Livy,' he agreed hastily, then finished his coffee in silence.

Livia suspected that he'd decided on silence as the safest course in the face of her sudden impatience and tendency to snap. And she hadn't been very nice, she acknowledged ruefully to herself. Still, it wasn't easy to deal with her feelings without giving them away. The balancing act seemed to be getting more difficult all the time, and she decided that Perry had been right when he had observed that she was in the middle of the winter of her discontent.

But her discontent grew even deeper when Dickon invited her out to dinner half way through the run of *Julius Caesar*. She went quite willingly, expecting to enjoy the evening. Dickon might be conservative and frequently dull, but he had a quick wit when he cared to use it. Good food and good wine (about which he knew a great deal, and which he always ordered for the two of them) tended to bring out the best in him, so Livia was prepared to forget her discontent for at least a few hours.

Instead, she got a protracted evening of Dickon's own discontent, and all of it centred on Jonathan. He wouldn't be back in time to start rehearsing on schedule. The location work wouldn't be done in time, and even if it were, he wouldn't come straight to Boston.

'He likes to go to parties,' Dickon said darkly, stating the obvious as though it were a new discovery.

'Then why can't he go to parties in Boston?' Livia asked with gentle humour. 'There ought to be plenty of opportunities. I'm sure Honey will do her best, even if all else fails.' She could afford to joke about it all, because she knew that Jonathan was not going to be partying when he came back to Boston, and Honey definitely wouldn't be a consideration for him.

'He's got something a lot more interesting than that,' Dickon explained with gloomy relish. 'He's stopping off to visit friends in San Francisco, on his way here.'

'How do you know?' Livia demanded.

'He told me. I got a call through the other night, and he said we probably wouldn't see him until the morning of the first rehearsal.'

'Oh,' said Livia faintly, attempting to digest all this. The first rehearsal was fine for the play, but it didn't precisely suit her. She wanted Jonathan back as soon as possible. She wanted a rather concrete demonstration of his feelings, and partying in San Francisco certainly wasn't it. She was more than a little abstracted during the rest of the evening, but Dickon didn't even notice.

Her abstraction lasted through the last few days of *Caesar*. The date of Jonathan's arrival seemed to be a source of endless speculation, but no one knew any more than Livia, and she knew nothing. Discontent seemed too mild a word for her feelings as she walked home one evening in a cutting wind which suggested January far more than March.

It seemed obvious that Jonathan had stopped to go to a party, she decided with something approaching despair, pausing on the last landing to search for her key.

'Well, thank God!' Livia heard the voice coming from the gloom at the top of the stairs.

'Jonathan?' she asked uncertainly, standing poised to retreat.

'That's right. I was afraid you might scream, or do something equally disruptive.'

'Why are you here?' She came more rapidly up the last few stairs, watching him unlimber his long frame and stand looming over her.

'Well, I didn't know where else to go, I suppose.' His voice sounded either flat or terribly tired.

'What did you do? Just sit here?' She hurried by him to unlock the door.

'There wasn't much else to do. But it's not especially comfortable.'

'Have you been waiting long?' she asked, switching on the light and turning back to see him properly.

'I don't know. I got in at some point this evening, and came directly here.' His eyes were narrowed against the bright light. 'There've been too many time zones, so please don't try to work the whole thing out.'

'You look positively awful!' And he did. It was hard to believe that his face could look more drawn and taut than it had when he had last been in Boston. But it did, and there were great shadows under his eyes, and an unnatural pallor to his skin.

'Yes, I expect so. You would, too, if you'd changed planes as many times as I have in the past couple of days.'

'Can I do anything?' she asked in an anxious tone.

'Let me sit down, for starters.' He walked stiffly into the living room, moving slowly and with great care, and then eased himself down on to the couch. 'Are you going to just stand there all evening?' he asked.

'No—I'm sorry.' She unbuttoned her coat and then laid it on the rocking chair.

He held out a hand and she took it and then, in

sudden alarm, laid her other hand over his. 'You're so cold! Don't you have a coat?'

'No. Never stopped to think of one when I was leaving—it was so damned hot. And I've been in airports or planes the whole time, until I got here. The only time I really needed one was coming here, to your apartment.'

'And while you were sitting on the stairs.'

'Yes. Well, it's not important.'

'It will be, when you get sick.'

'I never get sick. Right now I'm just tired to death. Look, will you please sit down? You're hovering, Livia.'

'I know,' she said softly. 'I'm worrying about you.'

'Oh, don't. Just sit down, please.' He searched his pockets until he found a crumpled pack of cigarettes and a lighter. As she sat down beside him she saw his hands shaking as he lit the cigarette.

'You aren't all right,' she said sharply.

'What? That?' He held his hands out, examining the slight tremor. 'That's nothing—just too much coffee and nerves and not enough sleep.' He smiled quizzically. 'You can be quite the little mother, can't you?'

'You can't help it if I'm concerned.'

'No, I can't. I expect that's why I came straight here. I remember the last time, when you offered to cosset me.' He smiled reminiscently. 'I need cosseting rather badly, right now, Livia.' He slipped one arm behind her and pulled her close. 'Oh, God, that's better. If you knew how many times I wanted to feel you! I began to regret my noble gesture, because it left me without anything to remember. There wasn't too awfully much to do out there, except remember things. And I didn't seem to have quite enough to remember—not the things I wanted, anyway. And that phone call—that was a farce, wasn't it?'

'You sounded as though you were enjoying it.'

'Of course I was. That was the whole point. I couldn't stand it any longer, by that time. I thought I'd reached the limit, which was silly, because it got a damn sight worse before I was through. But, at that point, I still had the energy to try to reach out to you. It wasn't terribly successful, though.' Jonathan paused, staring at the lighted tip of his cigarette. 'What I wanted was to have you there with me. You'll be happy to know that I kept telling myself that wasn't fair. No one ought to get dragged into that hole. My own fault that I got myself into the mess—no sense involving someone else. Am I making any sense at all?'

'I'm not sure,' Livia answered carefully.

'I didn't think so. The whole thing hasn't made any sense. You see, I've never felt like this before. I love you, Livia. I really do. I'm prepared to make a commitment—something I've never been willing to do before. In fact, I started on that commitment the night I left here. And the thing of it is, when one has started in on this commitment business, one ought not go off to a jungle half way around the world and leave the whole thing hanging. I've been feeling remarkably unfinished for the past three months. Is this all right to be saying?'

'Of course.' She laid her hand against his cheek and could feel the bone practically pushing through.

'I've got to be absolutely straight with you, Livia. I've got to be sure you understand everything—at least to the extent that I do. Because I'm not going to be easy to live with, even under the best of circumstances. And it isn't going to work at all, if you don't understand me.' He leaned forward to stub out his cigarette, brushing her hand away, unnoticed.

'You know I was married before?' he asked.

'Yes. Only vaguely, though. I haven't really followed you as a person.'

'She died in a car accident. That was about eight years ago. It made me into quite the tragic figure for a while. The grieving husband, trying to forget the pain—you'd know all about it, if you read the gossip columns. What none of them knew was that she was leaving me. Not for anyone else—just cutting out because she couldn't stand it any more. I guess she hadn't told anyone how she felt, except me, of course. Or, if she did, no one said anything about it. As far as people were concerned, we were a happy couple— although some people did wonder how she could be happy, what with my running around.

'That's why she was leaving, of course—that and the fact that she couldn't put up with my moods. It was my fault, I can't argue that. I was living very close to the edge, at that point—not that I've changed appreciably in the years since. But, on my own behalf, I will say that she wasn't exactly the warmest person in the world. I feel as though I might have changed, if she'd been willing to meet me part way. The whole thing made me feel a bit trapped. I had this constant sense of operating in a vacuum. There just didn't seem to be any points of contact. She'd never seemed to mind what I did. I'd about decided that I could go my merry way, being just as outrageous as I pleased. She didn't seem to mind, as long as the money was good and the status there, along with a certain amount of freedom to do as she pleased.

'That's why it surprised me so—that she wanted out. As far as I was concerned, about the first hopeful note in our marriage was that she minded my behaviour—the fact that I was, most assuredly, being less than faithful. I thought to myself, 'Well, by God, perhaps she does care.' But of course she didn't. She'd apparently gotten to the point of wanting nothing to do with me. We had a bit of a go around and she wouldn't budge. We were living in New York at the time, and she said she was going up to Connecticut to stay with some friends until she found a place of her own. So off she went, and the accident happened just outside the city.' He stopped, removed his arm from Livia's shoulders and lit another cigarette, leaning forward to rest his arms on his knees.

Livia said nothing, sensing that he wasn't done yet. He seemed so totally absorbed, caught by memories. She might have thought that he'd forgotten her presence entirely, except that all of this was obviously for her. And it wasn't coming very easily, either.

'I spent a bit of time wondering if she might have done it on purpose-unconsciously. There seemed to be two possible reasons for that. One, that she'd really loved me, after all, and couldn't stand the fact that it was actually over. The other, which rather perversely appealed to me more, was that she'd done it to have the final word—to make damn sure that I felt properly punished. Then I learned that some drunk had rammed her car—she couldn't have done a thing about it.' He shrugged. 'No hidden meanings, no great final act. Just fate, I guess.

'And the point of all this,' he continued, still brooding off into space, presenting Livia with nothing but a shadowy profile, 'is that I decided that the business of being close to someone wasn't for me. I'd tried it once, and it certainly hadn't worked. It seemed quite obvious, after the fact, that I'd probably quite deliberately chosen someone as incapable of closeness as I. I must not have wanted it, because I made damn sure that there wouldn't be any chance of it.

'So I've done as I pleased for the last eight years.

No one has suggested that I've had anything like a real relationship with any woman. They've come and gone so quickly that no one's been able to keep track. I certainly haven't. And then you walked into the hotel suite that day and I thought to myself, "My God, this is it." It was a bit like coming in out of the cold. I can't explain it. I just wanted to keep watching you—see what you'd do next.' Jonathan shook his head as though he didn't understand what he was trying to say.

'Actually, it didn't start at the hotel. It started when I saw that film of yours. First I thought that you were quite extraordinarily beautiful. There was that one close-up, and I was struck by those masses of dark brown hair, and the really remarkable contrast of your eyes. Green eyes, and so light against the rest of you that I thought, "There are eyes that can see anything. Couldn't hide a thing from eyes like those." And then the way you went about your business, and just took in that wonderful day and those trees—well, I can't explain it, but I could feel the strength in you. I knew you could handle anything.

'That's why it was so important to know that you hadn't been acting.' He turned to look at her and smiled gently. 'You see, I had to know if it was real. Because, if it was, it was what I wanted. You were what I wanted. And after the first few minutes, when you were a bit too sophomoric about me, you never missed a thing. I kept waiting for you to do something wrong, and you never did. God, I couldn't believe it, couldn't get over it.

'I don't expect that I'm explaining this very well. Perhaps I ought to list all your sterling qualities. You're good to look at. You've got a good sense of humor. You're intelligent. You never seem to mind, when I get out of hand. You've got this wonderful ability to put me in my place. You seem interested in getting to the *point* of me. Does this make any sense at all?'

It was a question he seemed to be asking frequently, in one form or another. This terrible need for reassurance was difficult to see. 'It does,' she said firmly. 'I do want to get to the point of you. Dickon said that you were open about everything but yourself, and that kept coming back to me. Most of the time he seemed absolutely right, and then you'd slip a bit, and I'd know he was wrong. And I'm not sure why it's so important to me that I decide what's real about you, but it is.'

'Well, it had better be, if you're going to marry me.'

'I hadn't been giving that aspect any thought at all.'

'I can't imagine why,' he observed, feigning confusion and wounded pride. 'I asked you at Christmas time. You've had two months to be thinking about it.'

'Oh, Jonathan! I wasn't taking you seriously that night.' And then, remembering some of his more revealing moments, when the loneliness had showed, she added, 'That is, I wasn't taking everything you said seriously. I certainly didn't take you seriously when you asked me to marry you.'

'Well, you should have. I think that was the whole point of the call—in my mind, at least. To make the declaration—get it out. Do something about that commitment of mine.'

'You might have said so. How was I to know?'

'Was I supposed to go on about how serious I was—that this wasn't just a passing fancy or a whim? I can just imagine how you'd have reacted to that, with your family hovering over the phone!'

'You could have made it sound just a bit more sincere, Jonathan. It seemed like a joke.'

'Did it?' He seemed to draw back at that and she felt

that he was searching for words. 'Does this mean I've been making a complete ass of myself tonight? Perhaps you'd rather that I hadn't brought all these things up.' There was uncertainty—real uncertainty—and doubt in his voice.

'No, it doesn't mean that.' She took his hand. 'It's just that you have had me feeling a bit like a yoyo most of the time. Back and forth, or up and down, constantly.'

Jonathan laughed aloud. 'Oh God, that's good!' Suddenly he pulled her close, wrapping both arms around her and settling her head against his chest. 'Poor Livia—the most composed and secure person I've ever known. Have I really been making you feel like a yoyo?'

'Yes,' she said defiantly, but it didn't come out that way, muffled as it was against his shirt.

'Poor girl!' He stroked her hair gently. 'We'll have to get rid of that uncertainty. Do you really want me? Will you have me?'

Livia nodded, not sure she could trust herself with words at this moment.

'All right!' He sounded triumphant now. 'I don't know the legal details offhand, but I can find out tomorrow. We've obviously got to have blood tests and do whatever has to be done to get the licence. I expect there's a waiting period. But it shouldn't take too long. I know that Dickon wants to start rehearsals on Monday, but we ought to be able to find enough time to pop off and get it done.'

'What are you talking about?' she demanded, pulling away slightly.

'Getting married, of course.'

'You surely don't mean now! Jonathan, be serious about this!'

'I am being serious,' he protested.

'But we can't!' She could feel his lips against her forehead, trailing down on to her cheek, which was not conducive to serious discussion. She twisted and put a foot of distance between them. 'Jonathan, we don't know each other well enough. We can't do this immediately.'

'Now it's my turn to ask what *you* are talking about,' He said almost icily.

'Look, I can count on the fingers of one hand the times we've had contact.' She began to list them. 'At the hotel, then at Dickon's party. Back here, that night or the next morning, or whenever it was. The next evening, after I got home from the theatre. That one telephone call, and then tonight—now. Well, that makes six, actually, so we're on to the second hand. But people simply don't get married after six encounters.'

'You said you wanted to marry me, didn't you?'

'Of course I did.' She reached out her hand and brushed the hair back off his forehead, wanting some closeness, some return of harmony. 'I do. But we can't do it instantly. We have to get to know each other better, or else we'll have a lot of rude awakenings.' She studied his face, hoping for a sign of softening, but she didn't find it. 'Jonathan, please! It just doesn't make any sense this way.'

'It made perfect sense to me.' The words were biting.

For the first time, Livia felt something other than conviction about her stand. There was considerable doubt creeping in, almost a sense of panic. 'Jonathan, people just don't do things this way—at least *I* don't. You can't expect me to do this in quite such a rush. There are things we'd have to plan. I have to give my family time. There's so much to think about.'

'You're going to refuse me because of your family?' He demanded.

'Of course not—and I'm not refusing you. I'm just saying that we ought to wait a bit.'

'I see.' He abruptly got up and stood towering over her, his face white. 'We've got to wait a bit, because *you* don't do things this way. *People* don't do things this way. My God, Livia, we're not people, we are ourselves. You say we ought to be sensible. Sensible! Perhaps I ought to have explained that I'm *not* a sensible person. I don't live by rules, by what other people think *ought* to be done. I thought I'd explained it. In fact, I thought that was much of the point of all I said tonight. But you didn't hear it—or you didn't understand it—so there doesn't seem to be much point in going on.'

'Jonathan, please!' she implored, standing up so she wouldn't be at quite such a disadvantage.

'Please? Please what? Play by your rules? And only by your rules? What are you—something out of an etiquette book?' He was absolutely livid and she could see a pulse beating furiously at his temple. 'Get to know one another better. Dear God, I know all about you I need to—at least I thought I did. Perhaps you're right—take more time and avoid rude awakenings. Well, I took a few minutes more than I thought I needed, and I certainly did have the rude awakening. I thought—well, it doesn't matter what I thought. You've heard it all, anyway, and it didn't make a dent. You like everything neat and tidy, don't you? God forbid you should find yourself doing something just a bit different.

'Livia, life isn't like that. You don't waste your time doing what you ought to do. You do what you bloody well have to do and need to do and want to do.'

'Yes, but you also have to be sensible, Jonathan. You really do.'

'Perhaps you do, but I don't and I couldn't be, even

if I wanted to. You keep right on being sensible, Livia. It's certainly served you well thus far. Twenty-nine years old and you've never been married. And your career—yes, that's been sensible, too, hasn't it? Creeping back to Boston to find a nice sensible place in a repertory company, where nothing can challenge you or disturb your placid little world. Perhaps you'd better withdraw from Dickon's play right now. Because there's the danger that it will disturb your placid, sterile little world. You're going to be noticed, you know. You're a damn fine actress, and the critics will notice that. God, what a thought! You might end up famous—you might be in demand. Then there would be decisions to make, Livia. And I'm not sure you can handle decisions. You seem to function better when there aren't any decisions.'

'Jonathan——' She tried again, pressing her hands together because they were trembling. Not that it seemed to matter—Jonathan wasn't going to notice. He was too angry; in fact, his voice was shaking with anger—or perhaps fatigue, she thought, wanting to give herself a bit of hope. 'Jonathan, please! You don't mean these things you're saying. You're tired——'

'Yes, I am. Are you going to offer me the universal panacea? Everything will look different after a good night's sleep? Oh God, Livia, don't be a greater fool, on top of all the rest. You ought to be looking at yourself, seeing what you're doing to yourself. And, quite incidentially, what you've just done to me.'

'I didn't mean to do anything to you,' she whispered, fighting tears.

'No, I don't expect you did. You haven't got a clue, have you? That makes it all the more remarkable. You ought to make a remarkable woman, in Dickon's play. You'll give the role a dimension Dickon never imagined. He thinks the man is the aggressor, the destroyer. He'll find out that the woman is giving every bit as good as she gets. Because that's how you'll do it—it's the only way you know how to operate. Watch out, Livia. You'll be great—if you do the play, that is.'

'Oh, I'll do it,' she snapped, suddenly stung to retaliation. 'You needn't worry about that. I'll do it to make damn sure you know you were wrong!'

He smiled thinly, a bitter smile. 'My dear, I already know I was wrong. But I've taken entirely too much of your time—and mine—as it is. And we really don't seem to have anything more to say to one another, do we?'

She wanted to cry out that of course they did, that they had to get this whole dreadful argument settled. They had to understand one another, each give a little. But there wasn't any time to say that, because Jonathan had turned on his heel and was walking quite firmly—and with dreadful determination, Livia saw—to the door. He slammed it violently behind him, and the sound seemed to echo in the apartment, echoing so loudly that she couldn't hear his retreating footsteps.

CHAPTER SIX

By Monday morning, Livia thought she might be tempted to melt at the first word or look from Jonathan. She had, by this time, decided that they would soon work out this conflict. Jonathan would see how unreasonable he had been. He'd realise that she was right and that his reaction had been out of proportion, the result of fatigue and nerves. It wouldn't take them long to patch things up. She was so confident of her judgment that she could approach the beginning of the play with composure.

Livia was the first to arrive at the theatre. She came in the stage door and went up on to the empty stage, where a long table, much battered and scarred, had been set up with a group of folding chairs around it. Otherwise the place was empty. She paced thoughtfully, seeing the stage with new eyes, as she always did on the day of a first reading. It was the same small and filthy place; still, on the day something new was about to start, it always seemed fresh and new. She felt an incredible sense of expectancy at a time like this, and cherished the chance to be alone, even for a few minutes, with her feelings.

Then, a few at a time, the other members of the company began to trail in and join her. There was a fair bit of milling around, and disjointed, random fragments of conversation filled the stage, echoing hollowly in the empty auditorium on the other side of the arch. Everyone seemed more than usually keyed up, waiting for Jonathan to appear. Livia doubted, though, that any of them were feeling the tension quite

as much as she was. She only hoped that she would
appear sufficiently composed when Jonathan finally
did arrive.

It proved to be considerably easier than she had
expected. At one moment the group was a vague and
poorly defined one; the next, it had coalesced around
the table, because Jonathan was suddenly among
them. He put down his script and peeled the top off a
paper cup of coffee, eyeing each member of the cast in
turn. It was a slow and deliberate examination, during
which no one said a word. Livia mentally braced
herself, as his eyes moved steadily closer to her. But
when he finally did make eye contact, there was
absolutely no change in his expression. It appeared
that he regarded her as no different from any other
member of the cast. His gaze moved on, leaving her to
wonder how long he would continue to treat her so
impersonally.

Once he'd got past her, she felt free to study him
with some concentration. It was a surprise to see that,
if anything, he looked better than he had the last time
she had seen him. She was trying very hard to be
detatched and analytical about him, but, just below the
surface, there hovered a wealth of feeling—most of it,
at this point, remorse.

'Well then,' he began, having finally made the
circuit of the group. 'As you can see, I'm here—in
spite of reports to the contrary. Sorry if I gave any of
you cause to doubt the timeliness of my appearance—I
really ought to keep away from foreign locations for
your sakes, if not my own. But I've made it, and that's
all that ought to matter. Now——' he looked around
quizzically, one eyebrow cocked, 'do you suppose you
could all contrive not to stand around like a herd of
cows?' And then, as people began to move into the
chairs around the table, he nodded. 'That's a bit

better—not having you all looking at me with bovine eyes. Perhaps if I sit down, you won't need to look worshipfully up at me.' And he let himself into the nearest vacant chair. 'You'll find that I'm rather peculiar about a few things—worship is one of them. You are none of you here to worship me, so—on the offchance that any of you had that in mind—please let it drop. We're here to work together, and I should like it to be an equal sort of thing, as long as you understand that I'm sort of first among equals.' He paused to light a cigarette. 'That's not because of anything special about me. It's because I'm going to be directing this play, so I'm going to have to impose my will, from time to time. I hope I don't have to very often, but I shall, when necessary. I don't want any of you to feel you can't argue a point with me. Just be aware that, when I say a decision is final, you'd better stop.'

He paused to sip his coffee, and that seemed to be a general signal to those who had brought their own that they could do the same. Livia, sitting diagonally across from him, poured coffee from her thermos, trying not to attract his notice.

'Now,' Jonathan began when people seemed to have settled in more comfortably, 'I don't know how you go about a reading, but I'll tell you what I like to do. I'd prefer to see you all read without any effort. You don't have to be completely expressionless, but don't try anything. Just read and don't feel that you've got to do anything with the lines at this point. In fact, I'd rather you didn't try to force anything. You might come up with the wrong thing and then we'll be stuck with it for a while. We'll read through this morning, break for lunch, and then read it through again, in the afternoon. That time you'll probably have a bit more expression, but it will be because you're hearing it for the second time. Just don't force anything. Clear?'

People nodded, and there was a general shuffle while scripts were got into place. Livia studied her copy for a minute, wishing that Dickon had found an easier way for her to begin the play. It started, at the opening of the curtain, with the two principals—Jonathan and herself—apparently in the middle of a conversation. It was going to be a difficult bit, because it was intended to give the impression of attempting to communicate. However, under the surface, the man was getting in sarcasm and hostility, while the woman was keeping herself withdrawn. Livia was relieved that she only had to read it this time—later would come the hard part of trying to make it real.

'All right, let's start,' Jonathan said at last, and went immediately into his first line. They went on for the better part of a page, passing lines back and forth. Then Jonathan stopped and sighed. 'Look, Livia, do you think you could keep the expression out?'

'I thought I was,' she answered mildly, surprised.

'Well, if what I'm hearing is being done with no expression, I'm afraid you're going to be over-acting, when you begin to add things.' He fiddled with his cigarette. 'Can't you just keep it flat?'

'Shall I try a monotone?' she asked, looking directly at him.

'Look, there's no need to get too flip about this. I'm simply asking you to keep the emotion down.' His tone was calm and reasonable, but there was a steely glint in his eyes. 'I expect you've spent a lot of time with the script, and have a lot of ideas, but I'd rather not hear them this morning. Either you've got a lot of ideas, or you're bringing a lot of excess emotional baggage to the part, and I could do without that.'

Some of the others were looking at Livia with

sympathy. Others were frankly staring at Jonathan, appearing either surprised or (in the case of the younger members of the cast) frightened. It was these reactions, rather than her own, which decided Livia that he was being unfair. Still angry about last week, she decided, and determined to take it out on me. Well, she'd give him his fit of pique, let him get it out of his system. There was no point in arguing or trying to read differently. Nothing was going to satisfy him, if he chose to be dissatisfied.

'I'll do my best,' she said steadily, and he nodded and took up where he'd left off.

After that one outburst there were no more interruptions. They read steadily through, heads bent over the script in concentration. Livia noticed that, when Jonathan was out of a scene, he occasionally studied those who were reading. There was a considering, calculating quality about his gaze, a measuring of strengths and weaknesses. She wondered if he watched her in the same way when she was reading.

When they were finally done, he leaned back and sighed. 'Well, that's over. It doesn't prove a thing, but at least you've all had the chance to hear yourselves in relation to the others. I, at least, find that I have a terrible selfconsciousness about reading aloud the first time. But it helps when I finally hear everyone else making asses of themselves—just as I am.

'Perhaps I'm telling you things you already know, in which case I'm sorry. I don't mean to condescend. I suppose I just like to hear myself talk!' He grinned. 'It's an interesting play. Staging is going to be fascinating. You notice that Dickon has given us precious little direction. He's called for a bare stage and Livia and I are supposed to spend the evening standing around. I don't think that's too practical—

Dickon ought to have realised that, sooner or later, one or both of us will start swaying. Then you'll have the whole audience watching that, instead of the action. I rather see it with the two of us on tall stools, or chairs of some sort, upstage. Then the only trick for us will be to avoid fidgeting or scratching our noses. I think, when we're speaking to each other, with no business involved, we should stay in the chairs. When it calls for action between the two of us, we'll come downstage. The rest of you, in your scenes, will just walk on and off. I haven't worked that out quite to my satisfaction yet. It would be nice if you could just appear on cue, in the lights, but I find that device awkward. People never do just appear when the lights come up on them. The audience always sees them sneaking on. So I've got to think about that.' He fingered his forehead absently, looking suddenly tired. 'And I ought to let you all get something to eat. Try to be back in an hour.' He dismissed them with a wave of his hand.

Livia was the last to leave, but it was not because she wanted to be alone with him. It was sheer bad luck—at least that was how she viewed it. She'd lost the top of her thermos at some point during the morning, and had to hunt around for a couple of minutes before she found it on the floor. When she emerged from beneath the table, she realised that she and Jonathan were the only two left on the stage. Jonathan was leaning forward, both arms resting on the table, staring blankly off into space. She wondered if he were recharging—he certainly looked as though he needed to.

She wanted to leave without saying anything, but she couldn't resist a human impulse. 'Aren't you going to eat?'

'What? Oh,' he looked up, 'I thought everyone had left. I'm sorry, Livia, I didn't hear you.'

'I asked if you were going to eat.'

'No. I'd rather like a little time to myself. Perhaps you could bring me back a sandwich, if that's possible—I don't care what. And coffee, too. I think, within the next twenty-four hours, I'm going to endow this place with a coffee machine,' he added. 'I don't fancy carrying a thermos, as you so foresightedly do, and I'm not going to get through this, without an unlimited source of supply.'

She nodded and walked off the stage, feeling quite impersonal about him, because he was certainly being that way about her. It seemed the best way to handle things at the moment.

When she came back from lunch Jonathan was still sitting in the same place, leafing through the script. She handed him a paper bag with his sandwich and a cup of coffee, and he nodded his thanks without looking up from the script.

'Dickon's written an awfully static play,' He said, taking the first sip of coffee. 'It needs a lot more movement than he's given it—which is characteristic, I suppose. Dickon's a very static sort of person. Have you ever noticed?'

'Many times,' Livia agreed, going around the table to take the same seat she had had in the morning. A few of the others were back from lunch but not yet at the table. They seemed to be giving Jonathan a wide berth, clustered at the far end of the stage.

'Lighting is going to be important, too,' he mused. 'I don't know a great deal about lighting. I hope the company has a good man.'

There didn't seem to be anything to say to that; he was merely thinking aloud.

'That's the trouble with simple plays. They're so much more difficult—so many more decisions to make. Ibsen is easy, from that point of view. One can have a good set, or an adequate set, or even a bad set, and it doesn't seem to matter much either way. But something like this takes a lot of thought.' He unwrapped the sandwich and began to eat, looking around and noticing, for the first time, the others gathered at the end of the stage.

'Oh, for God's sake!' he called, 'Don't stand over there. I can't abide that sort of thing—I told you this morning. Can't we talk about something? Have the courage Livia has. Just barge right up and start talking. Let's talk about the weather, or the possibilities for some night life in Boston.' He eyed them expectantly, with an almost calculating look, as they began to hesitantly take their places around the table.

Livia wondered briefly if he were calculating his effect on her or the others. There was no real way to tell; he went too fast. He seized the conversational ball and ran with it, leaving everyone trying madly to keep up.

'Night life ought to be a lively topic,' he mused, lighting a cigarette and squinting through the smoke. 'But Boston doesn't, somehow, seem like the liveliest of towns. 'Athens of North America'—that sort of place. Not that Athens was such a dull place, but I have the feeling that Boston is—all culture and no fun.'

'That's not true,' Honey put in quickly, with a calculating look of her own. 'There are lots of possibilities, Jonathan.'

'I expect there are for you,' he agreed with a grin. 'But then you've got lots of possibilities of your own. What do you do, Perry,' he asked, quickly turning away from Honey, 'when you want an evening on the town?'

'I usually don't have the money for an evening on

the town,' Perry answered almost apologetically. 'We don't get paid too awfully well, you know.'

'Good lord! You don't mean to say you let the lack of funds stop you, do you?' Jonathan shook his head with an expression of mock pity. 'I never did. I was once poor, you know—as poor as any of you. It didn't last long, thank God, and it's well and truly over now. But I didn't let poverty cramp my style. Poverty is nothing more than moderation carried to a deprived sort of extreme, and moderation has never been my style.'

'I know,' said Honey with a provocative flutter of eyelashes, but Jonathan ignored the thrust.

'Now Livia here——' he favoured her with a brief, almost challenging glance, 'I'd say that Livia is a decidedly moderate person, but she wouldn't carry it to a deprived sort of extreme. I expect that Livia doesn't run to extremes of any sort. And she'd rather I not talk about her like that, so I'll refrain.' This time he gave her a kinder look. 'I was a bit hard on her this morning, so I expect she's feeling the strain.'

He was silent for a moment, looking quite remote as he stubbed out his cigarette. Then, with visible effort, he resumed. 'None of you have been of much help to me in my quest for interesting evenings, but something will develop. Now, I expect, we'd better start again. You can put a little something into it this time,' he instructed. 'At least make it sound coherent. Dickon's got some nice rhythm in places. If you can hear it, don't be afraid to use it.'

Livia felt more comfortable this time. The play contained passages of verbal battling between the two of them, and she found herself enjoying these parts without selfconsciousness. Still, it wasn't easy, because much of what the man and woman had to say to one another cut a little too close to the bone. The anger

Jonathan was expressing, through his role, seemed all too personal to Livia's sensitive ear.

It seemed unfair, she thought resentfully. If he wanted to be truly angry with her (although she doubted that even Jonathan really knew what he wanted to do with her) she wished he'd do it on his own time, and not as a part of the play. She resolved to try to get a few things settled, before very much more time had passed.

It appeared that Jonathan had the same feeling, because, after the reading was finished and he had dismissed the cast, he asked Livia to stay on for a few minutes. So she remained in her seat while the others left. Jonathan appeared to be studiously ignoring her until the theatre was otherwise empty—leafing through his script with complete absorption. He kept her waiting even a few minutes longer—a sort of punishment before the fact, she thought. Finally he closed his script and looked up.

'I think we ought to talk, Livia, before things go any further. We're going to have to work together for the next couple of months, and it seems a pity to destroy whatever potential this play has, because of our personal feelings.'

'I wasn't intending to,' she said carefully.

'No, I'm sure that neither of us intends to, but we will, if we don't get a few things cleared up. I said, this morning, that you might be bringing a lot of excess baggage to the part, and that wasn't really fair. We both are, at this point. Somehow we've got to put what's happened behind us. The other night I made the mistake of indulging in excess, of putting personal feeling ahead of the work to be done——' He broke off and shook his head. 'I don't quite know what I'm trying to say. Right now I'm pretty well worn out, and I've got a splitting headache. There's no point in trying to settle anything right now—I'm not up to it. It's silly to suggest that we forget what happened, but I hope, perhaps, that we can at least ignore it while we work.'

'I was thinking the same thing,' Livia said quietly.

'Yes, well——' Jonathan stood up abruptly. 'Look, I'll try not to snap, and try to avoid little scenes like the one this morning. And it would help if you could try not to look so tentative about things.

'I don't know, Livia. Maybe we can work things out, after all. But not now—not in the middle of this. Let's just be friends for the duration. All right?'

But before she could make any reply, he'd turned and walked out. She watched him go, thinking that the sight of his back, as he left her, was getting to be an all too familiar sight. Perhaps that was characteristic. It might be the best he could do—come close to someone and then turn away.

CHAPTER SEVEN

DURING the first few days of rehearsal, Jonathan treated Livia exactly as he treated the other members of the cast. He seemed to have taken their last private discussion very much to heart. If he could not forget what had happened between them, he obviously could ignore it. He had suggested that they just be friends for the duration of the play, and it seemed that he was accomplishing that feat very well.

For Livia, just at first, it was not so easy. Jonathan might be able to laugh or joke quite impartially with her and the others, but she felt stiff and selfconscious in his presence. But each day became easier than the one before. His casual attitude, and the fact that she was treated exactly like anyone else, were obviously what she needed. By the fourth day she found herself able to exchange the occasional joke with Jonathan— not only behaving, but actually feeling that they were simply friends working together.

And it was on the fourth day that Jonathan— apparently having studied her reactions more closely than she had realised—decided that the time had come for the two of them to rehearse alone. At lunch time he dismissed the rest of the cast, explaining that there was no point in their standing around while he and Livia worked for the first time on the scenes which involved only the two of them.

After they were alone, he didn't give her a chance to retreat back into selfconsciousness.

'We could as well do this in your apartment or my hotel suite,' he observed immediately, giving her his best wicked grin. 'But I didn't think that you'd exactly go for that idea.'

'That's right,' she said sweetly.

'Of course, you realise that I can rape and pillage you just as easily here. Lord, I love that—did you really say it to Dickon?'

Livia nodded, and he laughed aloud.

'I wish I'd seen his face! It has such an untidy sound to it—must have really knocked him back on his heels. Look, I'd like some lunch before we start, but if we go out somewhere we're going to be noticed.'

'You're going to be noticed,' she corrected.

'Yes—at least for the moment. Your time will come. However, right now you can venture out and pick us up some sandwiches without attracting undue attention. Which makes you a "gofor". Once upon a time, before I was famous, but had every intention of being so, I vowed that I'd never have a gofor. It seemed a bit obscene—to be always sending people off to do what you could perfectly well do for yourself. Then, when I got famous (if that's what I am) I realised why the system exists.'

'To keep a bit of yourself to yourself,' Livia supplied, and he nodded. 'All right, I'll get the sandwiches.'

She went to the deli, taking longer than usual because she arrived at the height of the noon hour rush. When she got back to the theatre, she thought for a moment that Jonathan had left. The stage was empty and he wasn't to be seen in any of the seats in the audience. Then, in the dim light near the back of the auditorium, she saw his form, lying full length in the aisle.

'Jonathan,' she called tentatively, 'are you all right?' There was no response, and she let herself down off the front of the stage and flew up the aisle. 'Jonathan, please, are you all right?' she demanded breathlessly, bending down beside him on the floor.

'What? Oh, it's you. I went off to sleep.' He smiled selfconsciously and then the smile widened into a grin. 'I see I had you worried there for a minute. Thought I'd dropped dead, did you? *That* would have spoiled the play.'

'Damn the play!' she exclaimed, and then decided that was a bit too revealing. 'Do you make a habit of lying down in theatre aisles?'

'Not when I've come to see the performance— unless it's very dull, of course. But it's about the only place to catch a proper nap.' He propped himself up on one elbow and studied her face. 'I do believe you were worried.'

'It was unsettling.'

'Then I'll give you advance notice the next time. Now, let's eat the lunch you so kindly went for.' He smiled and got to his feet. 'And while we're at it, you can talk about the woman.'

'What exactly do you mean?' asked Livia, following him down the centre aisle, almost at a run.

'I want to know how you see her—how much you know about her. Dickon gives us some of it, with those scenes from the past, but the woman has to be a lot more than that. I'm interested to know what you've made of her.' He mounted the stage with one large stride and then turned to lift her up.

She felt breathless at being held by him, but it didn't seem to affect him at all. He held her only long enough to be sure she was securely on the stage and then released her.

'Now,' he directed. 'Eat and talk at the same time.'

She nodded obediently and began. 'I had a problem with her, at first, because it would be so foreign to me to have done what she did.'

'How do you mean that?'

'Dropping out of school at nineteen, just to get married. I was tempted to be impatient with her, because she didn't seem to even give a thought to the possibility of making a life for herself. But those scenes from the past helped. She really didn't have an opportunity to think of herself in any creative and independent way. I think the problem was that her parents had no imagination—never gave her any reason to consider new possibilities. Their crime was that they were too normal. If they'd been really cruel to her, if she'd had one of those classic unhappy childhoods, she might have chosen to rebel. But everything was just bland enough to keep her in the rut, so to speak. Once I'd figured that out, I could live with her.'

'You have some compassion for her?'

'Oh, yes. It seems a pity—she got into such a bad situation, married to the totally wrong person. The problem is that I feel some compassion for him, too. He's had much the worst time of it, and it does seem rather a pity that he can't reach out to anyone at all.'

'Ah, yes. Livia and her wounded bird syndrome.'

'What's that supposed to mean?' she demanded.

'Just that you seem to have an instinct for wanting to make people better, or to brighten up their lives. You played it on me, lord knows. You treat Perry like your son. And Dickon—you have far too much patience with Dickon, you know. He's an ass, even if he's also a good playwright. I can't imagine why you put up with him to the extent that you do. I expect you think he'll stop being an ass, some day, if you just give him enough support or reassurance. But that's a bit off the point,' he added hastily, seeing her about to explode. 'The point is that you can't have any compassion for the man—you shouldn't. The audience may, if it chooses—and it's my job to see that they do. You're not going to help me if you're running around the stage letting compassion leak out in your performance.'

'I wasn't going to play it that way.'

'I know that. Still, if the feeling is there, it's going to show, and we can't have that. You have no reason to feel compassion for the man. He's done a splendid job of ruining your life, and you're too involved in all that to have the objectivity to be compassionate. It's an interesting play because of that point: no sympathetic character—at least no character who projects a sympathetic quality. Dickon took quite a chance there. He wrote us both without a drop of the milk of human kindness, which gives the audience an opportunity not to give a damn about either of us. But he's giving them credit—and I hope they deserve it—for the ability to see the tragedy in these two lives.'

'I hadn't seen it quite that way.' Livia was silent for a few minutes, thinking through what he had said. 'I've got to be thoroughly passive, an icy bitch. And you've got to be agressively cruel. And then we let the audience draw their own conclusions.'

'Exactly.' He smiled. 'Do you see why we've got to keep the compassion out?'

'Yes.'

'It's a matter of control—in fact, I've never seen two parts which require more control. And I think yours is the harder of the two. I have the fun of being able to shout and bluster—some really terrific bits of anger. And you don't have that luxury. But you do get those wonderful moments, when your mind just disengages and you go spinning off into that place of your own. The audience has got to be able to see that.' He saw the flicker of concern on her face. 'You needn't worry—you can do it. You did it beautifully in that clothes line scene.'

'Yes, but that was on film, with a close-up. I can't do that for people far away.'

'Of course you can. You'll do it with more than your eyes. The whole line of your body is going to do it— the way you tilt your head, the angle of your chin, the way you shift your weight, your hands—I'll let you use your hands for that,' Jonathan grinned.

'You seem to have it all thought out,' she observed. 'Am I to take this as direction?'

'No, just observation. You'll find your own way into it and I'll correct you, if you get a bit off. I've seen you do it, you realise—at Dickon's party. You did it several times.'

'Did I really?' It was a reassuring thought—to know that Jonathan had seen her doing what she would have to do on the stage.

'Oh, yes. The first time was when I made that foolish announcement and you were so disapproving. You ought to have seen the way you were keeping space between yourself and me. It gave your body a wonderful line. The second time was when Honey began clinging to this vine—I've mixed my metaphors, haven't I? No matter.' He paused to light a cigarette. 'Anyway, that time you just removed yourself from the whole room, even though you were walking around and talking to people. It was a "well, she's gone, but we've got a piece of cardboard walking around in her place" sort of thing. The third time was when I came to take you home, while you were sitting on the couch. I'm not sure how you contrived that one, because you didn't seem to move a muscle—but I could see the pulling away, plain as day.'

'Do you notice everything?' she asked wryly.

'I try. One learns a great deal from it, in a general

sort of way. But I put a special effort into it, if I'm watching the woman who's going to be my leading lady in a play that's almost impossible. You'll do it very well. I'm not sure that you can do everything very well, but you certainly can do this. Dickon knew what he was doing.' He paused, eyes narrowed. 'I'm not sure if he likes either of us very much, from the look of this play. We seem to be two thoroughly unpleasant characters, don't we?'

'I suppose so,' she admitted. 'I hadn't really thought of it that way.'

'Well, it doesn't matter, does it? We've got work to do.' He stubbed out his cigarette and stood up. 'Come on, girl—you're about to start acting!'

And indeed she was. Jonathan took her through every one of their scenes together. At first it was disconcerting to Livia. When she was speaking, he would stand back, eyes narrowed, a completely objective observer. She felt exposed at those times, conscious of the things she wasn't getting out properly. Then, when he had a line of his own to say, he would suddenly be in character. A sort of controlled fury would come over him, and he would lash out at her, his voice menacing and bitter.

'How do you do it?' she asked finally, needing a break.

'Do what?'

'Go back and forth like that—be you and then the man, without even the slightest preparation.'

'It's control. I told you, this whole play is control. You've got to learn it, too.'

'Not the way you're doing it,' she objected. 'I don't have to weave in and out, so to speak. I should think you'd be exhausted.'

'And perhaps I am,' he said shortly. 'Do you suppose we could get on with it?'

'But I find it disconcerting—first I have you and then I have the man.'

'Well, you'd bloody well better get over that feeling,' he snapped. 'You don't have me, you know. All you've got is the man, and you've got to keep him in front of you, even when your director——' he spaced the words for emphasis—'is watching you. Now, I'm getting a little tired of watching you watching me, when I ought to be seeing nothing but the woman talking to the man. Do you suppose you could try to get it right?'

Livia was stung by his words, about to flare up, but thought better of it. Jonathan gave her the next line and she started off again, trying to blot out the sight of her 'director'. She was more successful than she'd expected to be, but that was because she was angry with him—hurt that he couldn't understand her problem.

'That's better,' he said, at the end of the scene. 'Only try to keep the anger out of your voice. The man's the one with the anger. You can't let the audience hear anger from you. They've got to hear resignation and some bitterness and cruelty, but not anger. You show anger only by withdrawing.'

She nodded and they went on to the next scene. She tried to keep the anger out of her voice and found the effort frustrating, because the anger was still there. It would have been a grand release to let it pour out. Still, perhaps he knew what he was doing, because she found herself working on gestures, needing some outlet for the feelings that were building up inside her.

'That's good,' said Jonathan at one point. 'The way you just knotted your hands together. They're not going to see the white knuckles from the cheap seats, but the force is going to show.'

She came out of character at his words and breathed a deep sigh.

'What's the matter? Finding it difficult?'

She nodded.

'Well, it's always harder to hold back—much harder than coming out with it. That's why it's such a trick to almost cry. I have to smile, when I hear people going on about how easily they can cry, on cue. No great trick to that—as long as you have tear ducts. But—to almost cry, to let the audience know that you want to, and are about to, and yet avoid that final self-indulgence of actually doing it—well, that takes courage and considerable skill. Control, if you like. The other trick is to go right back into character, to not let anything throw you off pace. Things happen on a stage. Things go wrong, or someone coughs at the wrong time, or some woman drops her handbag with a crash, and you lose the character for a second. So you've got to know how to get it right back, before you lose the thread of it.'

'I've been doing that for years.'

'Ah—you think so? You didn't hold it all the time, the night I saw you do Candida. Adequately, of course, enough so not many people would notice, but I saw it slip away once or twice. You haven't had enough discipline, that's your problem. Now, start again, where we left off.'

So Livia took a deep breath and started again, where they had left off. It seemed to go on and on—she hadn't realised before just how long the play was. She hadn't realised just how much she had to say, how many times they were just the two of them—tearing each other to shreds. She had the sensation that her world was shrinking until nothing existed except darkness and the looming figure of the man.

Rather near the end of the play came the one scene

she had been dreading for purely personal reasons. They'd done nothing more than read the scene through, before, so the physical contact which went with it was going to be new. And it was the physical contact that Livia had been dreading. First, according to the stage directions, Jonathan was going to put his hands on her shoulders, talk to her almost reasonably, trying to make contact. Then, 'They kiss' was all the stage direction said. Livia felt that those two words had the potential to cover a lot of ground. It was the one moment in the whole play when they both weakened, made some attempt to achieve closeness. After that Livia, as the woman, would try to pull away. Then, according to the directions, Jonathan was to 'take her with urgency' and Livia had spent a number of hours wondering exactly what that was supposed to mean. Take her how? With how much urgency? Jonathan hadn't been enlightening during earlier rehearsals. The first time they had done the scene, he had remarked, 'Well, we'll have to work on the action here, once we're a bit more in character.' They hadn't yet, and Livia suspected that working on the action was about to start.

They were standing about ten feet apart, downstage, and Livia gave him the line. 'Nothing seems to go right.' She turned to look at him, sensing that there had to be a certain softening in her attitude at this point.

Jonathan nodded, smiled briefly, and crossed the space between them. He looked down at her before he placed his hands on her shoulders. 'We haven't much to be proud of, have we?'

'No.' She studied his face, surprised at all the conflicting emotions she saw. What was acting and what was real? she wondered, just before his lips touched hers.

It started as a gentle, almost tentative kiss, and then she could feel the passion growing. His hands left her shoulders and she was drawn into his embrace, her lips parting under the pressure of his. Her hands had been motionless, but now, without conscious volition, they came up to caress him softly.

There had never been anything like this, she thought breathlessly. For an instant she was completely carried away from the play. Only Jonathan existed—Jonathan and her need for him. But simply admitting that thought was enough to bring the play back to her mind. She stiffened in his arms and her hands pulled away from the touch of his body. The action had nothing to do with the character or the feelings she was supposed to communicate. It was simply selfconsciousness, a feeling that he had caught her unawares and exposed her true feelings for him. She had to stop it somehow.

'You're not going to do that!' He said his line harshly, almost biting the words. Then he pulled her even closer, bending her body into his, forcing himself on her with controlled violence. He forced her lips apart again and kissed her deeply. One hand moved on her body with abandon, while the other arm kept her locked in his embrace.

Livia couldn't let her body relax, not even the slightest bit. She had to remain rigid, refusing to allow him to win. He was invading her, and she sensed that the only emotion left in him was anger. It was a question of violation now, and she had to resist.

'My God!' he finally cried, still using only the words Dickon had given his character. He pushed himself away from her, although his hands continued to dig painfully into her arms. 'You won't, will you? You won't give an inch. You don't have anything to give. You have nothing. You are nothing!' He thrust her away from him and turned abruptly.

And because he turned, he wasn't able to see the consequences of his act. Livia hadn't been expecting the force of his hands against her arms and was caught off balance. She was pushed back a step or two, her ankle twisted and she fell, hitting her elbow and skinning the palms of her hands on the rough boards of the floor.

'I was a fool,' Jonathan said, beginning his next line. Then he turned back, attracted by the sound of her fall. 'Good lord, did I do that?' he asked, abruptly breaking character.

She nodded, not trusting her voice.

'I didn't realise—I didn't mean—are you hurt?'

Livia shook her head and then decided that was a silly thing to do. She'd hit her funnybone, her hands hurt and her ankle throbbed. She thought that other parts of her body were also damaged, but hadn't been heard from yet.

'Are you sure you're all right?' He was kneeling beside her, looking decidedly anxious.

She sat up and flexed her hands experimentally. They smarted but appeared to move properly. She drew a long breath and then smiled. 'It's my pride, mostly.' She wiped at her eyes with the back of one hand. 'I didn't expect you to do that.'

'Any more than I did. And I didn't expect you to topple over quite so easily.' Jonathan smiled gently. 'I'd give you my handkerchief, if I had one.'

'Oh, that's all right. I'd have to wash it and press it before I returned it.' Then she laughed a little shakily. 'Am I going to have to do this every performance?'

'No, we'd better figure out something else. Look, can you walk?'

'Of course,' she answered with more assurance than she felt. 'Just let me be a bit slow about getting up.'

He helped her to her feet and she put tentative

weight on her ankle. It was sore, but it wasn't unusable. 'See? I really am in one piece.' And then, because he continued to look anxious and guilty, she smiled. 'We seem to be making a habit of hovering over one another this afternoon.'

'Yes, but you didn't do anything to me, as I did to you. I am sorry, Livia.'

'Oh, don't keep apologising,' she said airily, playing things lightly because he was still a bit too close for comfort. 'How was I doing, before you knocked me over?'

'Very nicely,' he answered, instantly diverted. 'I wasn't sure quite how to work that bit. I also expected you to be missish about it, but you weren't. We'll have to find some other way to get you out of my arms. Otherwise, I don't think I'd want to change anything.' He frowned, replaying the scene in his mind, Livia assumed. 'Why don't we quit for today! I expect you've had enough, and I rather think I have, too.' His face suddenly looked guarded or closed to her, as though something had displeased him.

Then he turned away, searching his pockets until he found a crumpled pack of cigarettes. Livia studied him, wondering at his quick change in mood. Two minutes ago he had been worrying over her. Then he'd been pleased with the scene. Now, suddenly, something had gone wrong; he was far away in some unhappy world of his own. It was strange—she was the one who had been battered, but Jonathan looked it, more so than she.

'Do you ever stay anything for very long?' she asked on impulse.

For a moment he didn't appear to hear her; then he frowned and turned to face her. 'What on earth are you talking about?'

'You. I think you must be the most changeable person I've ever known.'

'I do have my moods,' he admitted with a rueful smile.

'And there's another one,' Livia observed. 'I've seen four of them in about as many minutes. Lots of people have moods, but they tend to stick with one for a reasonable length of time. You certainly don't.'

'But then I'm not reasonable, am I?' This time he grinned, and Livia wasn't sure if he was baiting her or allowing her to bait him.

'Hardly. If I were going to describe you, reasonable wouldn't be the first adjective to come to mind. It wouldn't come to mind at all, in fact.'

'And what would?' He seemed to be seriously interested to know.

'Unreasonable. Mercurial. Outrageous and frequently infuriating.'

'That's all terribly flattering,' he said dryly.

'But I wasn't done,' Livia chided gently. 'I thought I'd get the worst ones out of the way first, and then go on to the ones you'd rather hear. You're fascinating— most of the time—and quite interesting to watch, from a distance, anyway.'

'From a distance,' he repeated. 'I hoped for a bit more than that.'

'Well——' she began, aware that the conversation had suddenly turned serious and deciding that she'd better be careful, 'I think, right now, that I've said about all I ought to.'

Jonathan nodded slowly. 'You're going to continue to hold that night against me, aren't you?'

'I'm not really holding it against you. But I think it takes a bit of sorting out, which I haven't managed to do yet.'

'No, I expect you haven't. And I can't say I blame

you, because I wasn't very understanding of your feelings, was I?' He studied the glowing end of his cigarette and then brightened. 'But I do think I'm behaving better—quite well, in fact, for me. Good behaviour is not exactly my strong suit, you realise.'

'I had noticed that.'

'I'm trying not to be quite so outrageous, and I've quite actively avoided infuriating you—at least, it's been my intention not to infuriate you. I expect I'll always be unreasonable and mercurial, though.' He flashed her his most charming smile.

'And I'm supposed to find that entrancing and appealing, I suppose,' Livia retorted more sharply than she had intended. 'You seem to think you can do just about anything you please, and I'm supposed to ignore it or forget it or just pretend that it didn't happen!'

'Couldn't you weaken just a little?' he asked, looking down at her with an arrested, almost puzzled expression. 'I need you, Livia. It's almost more than I can bear, sometimes—watching you and hearing your voice.' With one hand he touched her face, forcing her to meet his eyes. 'And perhaps I'm wrong, but I rather think you need me, too. But I'm not sure that you know that yet.'

'I do love you,' she said, against her will. 'But everything's gone all wrong, somehow. It would have been so easy, if you'd only been able to listen to reason, and wait.'

'That's better,' he whispered, and folded her gently into his arms. 'That's a start.' She felt his lips on her forehead. 'But you're wrong about one thing. It's not just that I wouldn't listen to reason, you know. There's a great deal more to it than that.'

'I don't know what you mean,' she said in a small voice.

'Of course you don't—not yet. You're awfully young, Livia. You must be the youngest thirty-year-old I've ever met.'

'I'm only twenty-nine—just turned twenty-nine, at that.' She tried to pull away, but he only held her closer.

'I know that, too. It just had more effect the way I said it.' She could hear the smile in his voice. 'Anyway, I love to see you flare up at me—it shows great promise. And you won't be so terribly young, by the time you're thirty, I can promise you that.'

'I expect I won't be young at all, by the time this play is over,' she answered, her voice muffled against his shirt. 'I wish you weren't so tall,' she complained, pulling away so she could look up at him.

'There's a way to correct that problem—to put us at an equal level.' Jonathan smiled the wicked smile and then kissed her expertly, his hands moving lazily against her body, stirring emotions she couldn't handle.

She locked her arms around his neck and felt herself lifted off the floor, so that he was holding her completely, her body moulded against his. The moment seemed to last and last; she was dizzy with the feel of him. And then he placed her carefully back on her feet and ended the kiss.

'You wanted me to stay with you, one night, and I refused. I think I've changed my mind.'

'No,' she whispered, and wondered why. 'Not yet.'

He nodded. 'I think you're right. I can't imagine why I'm being so bloody noble about you. Because I love you, I expect. You will be ready, some day. That's what I'm waiting for.' He kissed her once more, briefly and very gently. 'Now, for God's sake go—before I rape and pillage you!'

CHAPTER EIGHT

THE next morning, the entire cast was assembled for rehearsal—something Livia hadn't expected. She and Jonathan hadn't finished their scenes together, thanks to her fall. She'd assumed that they would finish in privacy, without the presence of the others.

'Feeling better?' Jonathan asked as she came on the stage. Then he turned to the others. 'Poor Livia had a bad time of it yesterday. I got carried away and threw her across the stage, and she went down with the most impressive crash. Not, I hasten to add, because she wasn't doing a good job.' He grinned. 'I expect it was because she was doing such a good one. And so must I have been, because I was quite thoroughly in character—couldn't stand her another minute, so I hurled her away. Now I've got to work out something a little less physical for that particular point. Livia says she doesn't want to get thrown at every performance. Have any bruises shown up?' he asked suddenly, turning back to her.

'I haven't looked.'

'Perhaps I should, later. With any luck at all, you've got them in interesting places.' He grinned suggestively and Livia wondered if he was playing to her or the others.

'Not very likely,' she said tartly, taking off her coat. 'If you're really interested, I'll give you a verbal report.'

'Put properly in my place, aren't I?' he asked the others. 'Here I have this grand reputation—unlimited success with women—and Livia won't give an inch!

Ah well, this is neither the time nor the place. Livia, we're going to start at the beginning of that last scene. Might as well give the others a chance, right now, to see how well it plays. And it will give me a chance to work out a suitable alternative to throwing you to the floor.'

'Right now?' she asked, incredulous. 'In front of everyone?'

He regarded her with amusement. 'Livia dear, I'm not sure how to break this to you, but the whole point of acting *is* to do it in front of people.'

There was a general murmur of laughter from the others. Livia thought that it was partly at her expense and partly out of sympathy for her.

'I know that,' she snapped. 'Just give me a minute.'

Jonathan nodded and lighted a cigarette while she turned away.

It wasn't going to be easy. Yesterday she'd had time to assume the character and had been ready for the scene when it came. Also, they'd been alone; she realised that had helped enormously. It was a very personal and revealing moment in the play and, to make things even worse, it seemed to say as much about their personal relationship as it did about their relationship as characters in a play.

She felt a moment's panic, realising that everyone was waiting, watching her, expecting her to leap into character and come out right. She had to block them out; she had to block out everything but the feelings she'd had yesterday, when nothing had existed but the darkness and the man. She ran back through some of what ought to have come before—fragments of misunderstanding and hostility. She felt the rigidity, the cold control of the woman coming over her.

'All right, I'm ready.'

'That didn't take long,' Jonathan noted approvingly,

stubbing out his cigarette. 'Now, before we start, I want to show you what I propose to do at the end, so that you don't fall. I'll have my hands so—on your arms.'

'You might have thought of this before I went to all the bother of getting into character!' she flared, but he only smiled.

'I'll have my hands so——' And he gripped her arms, his fingers digging in just as painfully as they had the previous day. 'Then, instead of just pushing you away—which is how I got you into the mess—I'm going to take this hand away.' As he removed one hand, she thought for an instant that he was going to strike her. He must have been reading her face, because he nodded. 'That's right, that's what you're supposed to think. But then, with my other hand, I'm going to turn you slightly. You see, I don't want to hit you, so I've got to get you out of range. So I spin you around and then I release you and you're going to go flying off—about six steps or so, I should say. But you've got to be ready for it, so you can keep your feet under you. Now,' he directed, 'try it.'

He placed both hands back on her arms, fingers still digging in. There were going to be a few choice bruises there, she thought. Then one hand came up, and almost immediately she felt him turning her, forcing her off. It was a decided push, although not quite so unexpected or as strong as the previous day's push. She started back, fighting to keep her feet under her, finding that it took more than six steps before she regained her balance and could stop.

'Well,' he said, 'that's not bad for a first try. A bit too much, don't you think? We've got to stay away from melodrama here. Try it again, and take a few less steps.'

'That wasn't dramatic effect,' she protested, coming

back to him. 'That's how long it took before I could
stop. Perhaps you could shove me off with a little less
violence.'

Jonathan nodded and they started again. It took
four tries, before he was satisfied. The others watched
silently, slightly in awe. 'That's good,' he said at last.
'I like the way your hand came out, at the end. It
makes a nice line. Do that every time, will you?'

'Easy for you to say,' Livia retorted breathlessly.
'I'm just trying to keep from going down again!'

'And that,' said Jonathan to the entire group, 'is
why ballet lessons are a good idea for actors. Learning
how to use your body properly, with grace and
authority. Have you taken ballet, Livia?'

'Not for years. It doesn't seem to have helped. I
wouldn't mind throwing you across the stage, just
once, so you could see what it's like.'

'You couldn't.' He eyed her for an instant and she
knew he could see her anger and steely determination
growing. 'That is, it's not part of your character. I
have every confidence that you could do it—if I were
willing to let you.'

'Or even if you weren't,' she snapped.

'Well, we can argue that point later. Now we'll do
the scene.'

And they did, starting with Livia's line, 'Nothing
has seemed to go right.' When he first kissed her, she
was unable to resist, just as she had been the day
before. And then, as she had before, she began to
resist and withdraw. She felt the same sense of
indignation and sense of violation. Jonathan pushed
himself away from her and delivered his bitter lines.
Then, as they had practised, his one hand came up,
while she tried not to flinch, and then he spun her
away. She wasn't consciously counting steps, but she
knew that she took only five before regaining her

balance, half turned away from him, her hand out, as though grasping for something to hold her.

For an instant, as she looked at him, she saw only the man, furious and almost revolted, his body stiff with controlled fury. Then, suddenly, the tension was gone and Jonathan was back, smiling appreciatively. 'Now that was very nice. That's what this play is all about. Don't you think so?' he demanded of the others who were standing around the edges of the stage.

There was general agreement, although it was restrained. Livia sensed that the restraint had nothing to do with doubts about the scene. It seemed, rather, to be a gradual coming out of absorption with the action. They'd been caught by it, she decided with a sudden surge of confidence. They'd been drawn in and as moved as she might have been, had she not been a part of it.

She felt tears in her eyes—a silly thing, and she tried to make them stop. But there was something overwhelming about the reaction of the others, and Jonathan's brief approval. The knowledge that she had done something fine was almost frightening and certainly moving.

'What's the matter, Livia?' Jonathan asked, studying her face. 'Did I hurt you after all?'

She shook her head, not yet trusting her voice.

'Ah. Finding it a bit harder than you expected?' He sounded almost sympathetic. 'That's what happens when you work harder than you know you can. Takes a bit out of you, doesn't it?'

'Yes, it does,' she agreed, blinking away the tears which fortunately hadn't fallen.

'Right. Well, now you get to rest for a few minutes.' He smiled briefly and then turned away. 'Can I have people out here, please?' he called to the rest, and started rehearsing them, while Livia collapsed in her chair.

'Takes a bit out of you,' he had said, and Livia had to agree with that statement. She felt as empty now at the end of that one brief scene as she had ever felt at the end of an entire play. She hoped it got easier, as one became more accustomed to this level of work. Certainly Jonathan didn't seem to be affected. He was pacing, listening to Perry and Honey and occasionally stepping in to correct a delivery or to offer suggestions on movement or position. Inexhaustible seemed the best word for him now, and she wondered how on earth he did it. It wasn't the moving around that filled her with awe. It was, rather, the way he could put himself into a scene, use all the right emotions—spend himself, she could only assume, as she spent herself. Then, having done all that, he could drop it, without appearing to miss a beat, become himself, and get on with the business of directing others. There must be something quite wrong or inadequate about her, she decided. Here she sat, like a limp rag, while Jonathan went on as though nothing remarkable had happened.

Most assuredly he was a more experienced actor than she; perhaps it all came more naturally to him than to her. Or possibly—and this thought was a fusion of what Dickon had said and what she had sometimes thought—he hadn't any sense of himself. She wondered if acting—the doing of it, the working at it, the sharing of it with others—was all he had. But that was a thought she couldn't pursue at this point. If she wanted to survive this kind of work, this sort of intensity, she had to keep all private feelings out of her life. And besides, Jonathan was ready for her again, she realised with a start.

'Back to work, Livia,' he called. 'Now you've got to wander into this scene—not actually into it, but on to the fringe of it. It becomes a part of your memory, although it's been mine from the start. You come downstage where Dickon indicates in the script, and stand just behind Honey and Perry. I'll be here——' He walked to the far side of the stage and stood for just an instant, arms folded, staring intently at the two younger players. 'Now Honey and Perry exit——' he dismissed them with a wave of his hand—'and we have our last crack at one another. You start off.'

'We haven't done anything but walk through it,' she objected.

'That doesn't matter. You've got the feel of the part quite nicely, I should say. Just take it through and we'll worry about corrections after we're done.'

'Yes, but I've got a few questions——'

'Save them. Perhaps you'll find the answers.'

So Livia started off, wondering rather wildly if she had any reserves left to summon. She still felt drained, and the scene demanded touches of compassion and regret, a wealth of feelings that had to gradually slip away until there was nothing left. At least that was how she thought it ought to go for her, but she wasn't sure. That was what she had wanted to discuss with Jonathan, before they started. It didn't seem fair to do the scene before she knew what she ought to be doing. She felt even more unequal to the challenge because she was starting flat, when she ought to be starting with emotion which trailed gradually off to flatness.

She sensed that she was blundering through the scene, making obvious mistakes all along the way. Jonathan, on the other hand, was a marvel to behold. He seemed to have it all—not even her mistakes threw him off his stride. At the very end, with the curtain speech, she found him absolutely dazzling. Before, when reading the script or walking through, she'd seen his last speech as bitter and filled with anger. And so it was, but the amazing thing was how he delivered it. There was an incredible absence of emotion, a restraint and resignation in his voice and his gestures. He didn't seem to have the ability to care any more, even though the words he had to say were powerful.

It left her breathless, with a glimmering of what real greatness was. It was, quite simply, the ability to take something obvious and turn it into something unexpected, something personal and terribly real. And because of what she'd seen and heard from Jonathan, she was hardly aware that the play had ended.

Even Jonathan was still, when it was over, and he seemed to have to make an obvious effort to shake off the mood. 'Well,' he finally said at last, beginning to hunt for yet another cigarette, 'you certainly got the last of it awfully wrong.'

'I told you I had questions.'

'And you didn't seem to find any answers, did you? You've got a good rhythm to work with, but you aren't using it. Start off slowly, build emotion, flirt with involvement and then withdraw slowly.' He shook his head. 'You aren't supposed to hear any of what I say at the end, you know. You tune me out completely at some point—you'll have to decide when.'

'That's what I wanted to ask,' she told him, trying not to feel that she was being treated unfairly.

'That's what I thought you'd know for yourself.'

'Well, you're the director,' she accused.

'And you're supposed to be an actress. Tell me, do you think you're going to have enough energy to sustain character through three full acts?'

'I know I will.'

'Do you?' he asked with a sardonic smile. 'That rather surprises me; you certainly didn't produce it just now.'

'That's because I'd never done it before.'

'You'd never done it before,' he repeated. 'And I

was under the impression that you'd been acting for a number of years. Someone ought to have warned me that I was going to be working with a green girl!'

'I am hardly a green girl,' she snapped, drawing herself up. 'But I'm afraid I don't have your advantage. I'm not slightly mad around the edges, and I don't play with people—all soft and sweet one moment, and rude and insufferable the next. You——'

But before she could say another word, Jonathan had taken her arm roughly and marched her across the stage, as far away from the others as possible.

'Would you kindly keep our personal affairs out of this?' he hissed. 'I'm trying to get a performance out of you, and it's obvious that I'm not going to get it by being all soft and sweet, as you put it. Perhaps last night was a golden moment for you, and you thought it was going to last, but you're quite wrong. And you may think me mad, if it pleases you, but you're quite wrong about that, too. I know exactly what I'm doing. Now, do you suppose you can go back into this and do the sort of job I think you're capable of doing?'

Stung, Livia pulled herself free from his grasp and marched back to where the others were standing uneasily. They had obviously been wondering if they ought to be listening or ignoring the small battle that had just taken place. Facing them, looking far more composed than she was feeling, wasn't the easiest thing Livia had ever done. It did have the attraction of leaving Jonathan alone at the far end of the stage and, she hoped, at something of a disadvantage.

It didn't seem to. He waited a few seconds and then ambled back and quietly told her to start the scene again. He made her do it over and over, while the others watched. Grudgingly, Livia had to admit that perhaps he did know what he was doing, although it didn't change her opinion that he was a bit mad around the edges. He'd certainly mobilised her, got some energy back into her performance. It was anger that he'd given her, of course, but she found that she could use the anger quite effectively. She could twist and mould the anger into what she felt she ought to be doing.

But Jonathan kept after her, criticising, correcting, coming down on her with special vengeance at the very end. He continued to insist that she must not even hear the very last things he said to her, and he continued to be convinced that she was hearing him. He was right, of course; she was hearing him. It was difficult not to hear such a brilliant piece of work. What she found most fascinating was that he changed things slightly, every time he did the scene. The basic structure of his first delivery remained, but the shadings were always different. Sometimes he added more anger or resentment, or even more resignation. And once—the best time, she decided—he had visibly forced himself to find the energy to say anything at all to her.

It was the finest bit of acting she had ever seen. What made it great was that every version was right, even though each was right in a different way. She wondered if he'd keep it up, keep changing the delivery every night, after rehearsals were over and they were performing for the public. It was, to say the least, disconcerting. Jonathan kept at her, insisting that she should not listen, and then kept producing something she could not help but hear.

Finally he gave up. 'Let's quit for today. Livia doesn't seem able to get it right, and I'm getting tired of it. I expect the rest of you are, too—standing around and watching her ruin things.'

'If you'd settle on one reading, I'd stop listening!' she told him sharply.

'And I'll settle on one reading when you stop listening,' he answered with deceptive mildness.

'Is this to be a battle of wills?'

'I shouldn't think so,' he answered consideringly. 'But you can't expect me to settle on something until I know how you're going to be reacting.'

'And I might say the same,' she pointed out with some heat.

'No, that's not valid. All you have to do is not hear me—as I've told you countless times. I need to know how you're not going to hear me.'

'I'm just not going to hear you, that's all. I think you're just having a tantrum, and all *I* need to know is how long it's going to last.'

He smiled briefly. 'Nice try, Livia, but it isn't going to work. Now for God's sake, go home. I'm getting tired of looking at you.'

In the days that followed, Jonathan drove them all unmercifully. They rehearsed daily, almost without breaks. Lunches were grabbed on the run, and days didn't end until later in the evenings. Livia didn't know what the others did about dinner; she went home each evening and ate canned soup before throwing herself into bed. Even weekends provided no relief, because they didn't exist for Jonathan. The play was all-important, and nothing was going to stand in the way of his quest for perfection.

Given this single-minded approach, his announcement on the third Friday of rehearsals came as something of a shock.

'Go home, children,' he instructed, glancing at his watch as they reached a logical pause in the action. 'You've all been behaving very nicely indeed, and I think it's time I threw a small crumb in your direction. You needn't be back until Monday morning. Get plenty of sleep and just forget about this whole bloody business for a couple of days. But don't think that I've gone all soft, because I haven't. I simply don't want the lot of you dropping from nervous exhaustion. Things are going well, you've earned the rest, and I expect you all to be fresh as the proverbial daisies on Monday. Then we can all make that last effort for the opening—which, I need not remind you, is only six days away.' And then, almost before his words had registered, he was out of the theatre, leaving the others to depart in his wake.

Livia, finding it something of a novelty to be leaving the theatre before dark, walked slowly home. Jonathan had actually dismissed them at a quite rational hour— so rational, in fact, that there were still plenty of other people heading home. Near her apartment, she met Maureen, and thought wistfully that here was a person who got home at a rational hour every night.

'I haven't seen you in an age,' Maureen remarked, falling into step beside Livia. 'I hear you, some nights, dragging in at the most ungodly hours.'

'They've all been ungodly,' Livia sighed.

'Does that mean it isn't going well, or that you're having a passionate affair with Jonathan Worth?' Maureen asked impishly.

'It doesn't mean *that*,' Livia said shortly. 'He's an absolute tyrant, and he believes in working people to death. But now he's afraid that some of us just might go and die on him, so he's sent us all home early and given us the weekend off.'

'Than I gather it hasn't been quite the bed of roses we were imagining it to be?' Maureen asked a little more seriously.

'I never imagined it was going to be a bed of roses,' Livia corrected. 'But I didn't know it would be quite this bad.'

'Isn't it going well?'

'I think it is—now. But it hasn't been easy. We've had some pretty intense battles about one thing and another.' And that, she thought wildly, was the understatement of the year! 'But I'm getting better, and he's getting less abrasive, so I guess we'll both survive.'

'Was there ever any real danger that you wouldn't?'

'Not really.' Livia smiled a little sheepishly. 'At least, there might have been, about me, but Jonathan can survive anything. He's quite single-minded when it comes to acting—absolutely nothing is ever permitted to get in the way of that. It shows, too, because he's such a master. The funny thing is that he's beginning to get some of the same sort of stuff out of me. I don't mean,' she added hastily, as they entered the apartment house, 'that I'm as good as he is, but I'm better than I've ever been before.'

'Then he must be a good director,' Maureen observed with more perception than Livia expected.

'Yes, he must be, although I'm not sure quite how he does it. He never tells me what to do; he just keeps asking me, over and over, why I'm doing what I'm doing. I have to justify everything and, when I can't, I know I'm in trouble—that what I'm trying isn't working. So then I try something else, and it's usually better. I used to fight with him over all these points, but it didn't work. So I don't fight anymore, and I keep trying new things, and I do keep getting better. It's quite amazing, really,' she added with a sudden burst of enthusiasm she wouldn't have thought she had the energy to produce.

'But there's no great romance?' Maureen asked almost sadly.

'None at all,' Livia assured her grimly. 'Any actress who can manage to work with Jonathan Worth *and* share a great romance, all at the same time, has got to be some sort of an acting marvel. And I am obviously *not* an acting marvel. I'm just hanging on for dear life.'

'That's a shame. I did have great hopes. Still,' Maureen added, brightening, 'you open next week and perhaps things will settle down. You might have the time and energy then to really get involved.'

'I wonder.' Livia breathed a sigh, completely oblivious to her friend's curious look. 'There just isn't time to think about anything like that. I expect that I'll look back on all this some day, and realise what a glorious experience it was, but not now. Right now, I just want my bed.'

She left Maureen on the second floor landing and went up to her own place, where, after the usual can of soup, she fell into bed and went instantly off to sleep.

She came back to consciousness some indeterminate time later, although it seemed like only minutes to her. There was a noise, an intermittent but insistent one, which she first thought was the alarm clock. But she hadn't set the alarm clock—even half asleep, she could remember that.

It was the telephone, and she lay there waiting for it to stop ringing, so that she could go back to sleep. But the foolish thing wouldn't stop; someone was determined to make her answer.

She went barefoot down the hall and picked up the phone. She fully expected a telephone salesman, but instead it was Jonathan.

'Good morning,' he said so brightly that she wanted to murder him.

'What time is it?' she asked, pushing back her hair. 'I was sleeping.'

'It's eleven, and I expected you would be. Some of us are much better at sleeping than others.'

'And I was doing awfully well, until you called.' She

sat down on the chair beside the phone and rubbed her eyes. 'Don't tell me you want to rehearse some more.'

'No. I wanted to point out that spring has arrived in Boston. Possibly it arrived days ago and we were all too busy to notice. But it's certainly here today— seventy degrees and lots of sunshine. I thought we'd have a picnic.'

'Do you realise how disgustingly alive you sound? And how depressingly dead I feel?'

'You don't sound too good, that's true. Perhaps you've been working too hard. But think how much better you'll feel in fresh air and sunlight, with good food in you. You see, I'm the one who's been working you so hard, so it's obviously my responsibility to give you a little rest and recreation.'

'That's what I was having, until you called,' she told him.

'Do you always wake up in this frame of mind?' Jonathan asked. 'What you ought to do is have a good strong cup of coffee and a bracing shower. I'll be along in about a half an hour. I assume you know some place out in the country where we can go.'

'I don't know any places in the country. We can walk to the river.'

'Then I've won, have I?'

'I suppose so,' she admitted ungraciously. 'I can't think why.'

'It's my fatal charm.' She could hear the grin. 'And look, you don't need to put together a lunch—the hotel is doing it for us. I'll see you in thirty minutes.' And before she could say anything more, he had hung up.

Livia supposed he arrived on time. Because she hadn't known what time he had called, and hadn't had the sense to look at the clock after she hung up, she couldn't be sure. She was ready, but only barely—hair still damp from the shower and wildly unmanageable. She tied it back with a scarf and put on an old pair of jeans and her only clean jersey. Not very imaginative, but the best she could do on short notice.

'You know,' Jonathan began, as they started down the stairs, 'we may have a problem, if I'm recognised.'

'You shouldn't be so conceited! No one's going to recognise you today. No one's going to expect you to be having a picnic by the river with such a plain little thing as I.'

'I don't think you look all that plain,' he said appraisingly, as they stepped out into the sunlight. 'Are you always so compulsively correct with your pronouns?'

'I wish you wouldn't dart from subject to subject, while I'm not completely awake!'

'Sorry. I'll ask you about pronouns later. Shall I stick to the subject of your plainness?'

'I'd rather you stuck to nothing at all, at least until I get waked up.'

He took her at her word and said nothing, while they walked slowly along in the spring sunshine. Perversely, that irritated her—that he should be so obliging. She risked a brief sideways glance at him and found that he was ignoring her completely. Or rather, she corrected, it appeared that he was ignoring her completely. He was wearing large dark glasses, the reflecting kind, so there was really no telling what he was looking at. Still, he wasn't looking down at her— she still found it strange to be with someone so tall that she had to be looked down upon in such a decided way.

She chanced another, longer look. He seemed quite strikingly handsome today, and definitely theatrical. His hair was a glossy as a raven's wing. His deep blue glasses almost shrieked 'star!' and his clothing—a turtle-necked black shirt and close-fitting slacks—did everything possible to emphasise his tall leanness. But the most theatrical touch of all was a gold chain around his neck, with a heavy medallion of some sort suspended from it. The sum of the parts made for a startling effect; all dark blue and black, with a pale face which suddenly seemed not to have so many planes and angles in it. It was like suddenly looking at a stranger's face, and yet it had once been the only face of his she had known. It was, she realised, his stage face, the one she had watched from a distance, when she had seen him perform on the stage. Good lighting—or sunlight—certainly had the power to change him, and Livia wasn't sure how she felt about that discovery. Over the past few months she'd grown quite accustomed to the poorly lighted and well worn face which had the advantage of allowing emotions to show.

They had come, by this time, to the bank of the river. Jonathan paused and surveyed the broad expanse of grass which was littered with people.

'Lots of others seem to have had the same idea.'

'Always, on a weekend day like this,' Livia agreed. 'It's frightfully important, you see, to start working on a tan as early as possible.'

'And some seem to be working with more dedication than others.' He eyed two young girls stretched out on a blanket, displaying most revealing bikinis. 'I should think they'd freeze. It's not that warm, do you think?'

'No, but there are times when a girl will do anything for the perfect tan.'

'You sound as though you speak from experience,' he said, and turned his head so that the mirrored glasses appeared to be looking at her.

'Oh, I am. My dorm wasn't far from here, and we

used to come over and rub ourselves with a mixture of baby oil and iodine. Most bizarre, but we believed it gave the quickest tan.'

'So you once did bizarre things,' Jonathan said musingly. 'That's good to know.' And then he took her hand and led her through the maze of sprawled bodies and casual games of ball or frisby, until he had found a relatively empty spot. 'Perhaps we'll be a bit off-putting,' he remarked, unstrapping a blanket from the side of the picnic hamper. 'We're much too conservatively dressed, and I'm afraid the hotel has provided us with a lavish spread—more than one would expect to find here. Do you suppose all these children will decide we're snobs and keep their distance?'

'I wouldn't call them children, precisely,' Livia said doubtfully, but Jonathan shook his head.

'Perhaps you wouldn't, but I've got a good twenty years on most of them—or else they've got a good twenty years on me. I expect it all depends on whether one appreciates youth or age.'

'You aren't ancient, you know.'

'No?' He cocked an eyebrow in disbelief. 'You drop me down among this group and I feel it. The old joints are creaking,' he added, lowering himself on to the blanket. 'And there you are, looking absurdly like a schoolgirl, with your hair tied back like that.'

'I'm hardly a schoolgirl!'

'I know that, even if you do look like one, from time to time. A trait I expect you'll no longer have, when I'm done with you.' He grinned, but Livia found it not quite what she was accustomed to seeing. His eyes were so uncompromisingly hidden by the glasses, making his face and expressions incomplete. 'Well,' he added after a pause, 'since you won't rise to that bait, do you want to eat?'

'Lord, yes. Do you know, when Dickon said we had two whole days off, all I could think of was the chance to sleep for hours and then eat something real for a change!'

'What do you mean by something real?' he asked idly, beginning to take things out of the picnic hamper.

'Oh, anything that wasn't canned soup or a cardboard sandwich from a take-out counter. I've been living on the cutting edge of malnutrition for the past few weeks.'

'Will this help?' He was carefully laying out cutlery, plates and interesting containers.

'You're being awfully domestic,' Livia observed, and then added artlessly, 'I think you're trying to please me.'

'Oh, I am—very seriously. I can't think why I chose this form of expression, though. I loathe sunlight and I'm not particularly fond of fresh air. But you seem like the sort of person who likes both of those—just as you're the sort of person who has a home to go to for Christmas. And so—besotted fool that I am—I decided that a picnic seemed the right sort of thing to offer you on a day like this.'

Livia thought it prudent to avoid any comment on what seemed to be a rather revealing statement, so she began to look through the silver-plated containers. 'Do you always have pâté at a picnic?' she asked with real curiosity, because she'd never before seen such an exotic collection of food served on the ground.

He smiled selfconsciously. 'I must confess that I don't ever recall having gone on a picnic before, unless one counts those mass productions put on by schools and summer camps.'

'Never been on a picnic?' she asked, incredulous. 'You certainly found a super way to begin!'

'I'm not sure I like the sound of that,' he observed. 'It implies that you expect me to continue this practice of picnics, and that wasn't my intention.'

'I know. You loathe sunshine,' she nodded, beginning to select from the rather dazzling array of food. 'Is that why you wear those dreadful sunglasses? To keep the sun out?'

'No. What I dislike about sunlight is that one is expected to function cheerfully, just because it happens to be a sunny day—which seems to me to have nothing at all to do with how one actually feels about life at the particular moment. The glasses were an attempt to avoid recognition, although I expect you to tell me again not to be so conceited.'

'Oh, I've got a greater objection than that. They reflect, so that I can't tell if you're looking at me or something else entirely. And besides, it's most disconcerting when I look at you, because all I see are two rather bulbous reflections of myself.'

'But I am looking at you—rather constantly. Even when you were taking those covert glances at me, on the way over here.' Jonathan smiled and pulled the glasses off. 'There. You see?'

And she did. Even with his eyes narrowed against the sudden increase in light, he was watching her with a considering and very serious gaze. 'That's an improvement,' she said. He looked more like the self she now knew, but he was still disconcertingly different. The planes and angles were less pronounced, washed out by the sun. But fatigue showed in other ways—in dark smudges under his eyes and in a certain taut, carefully held quality about his features.

'I slept thirteen hours or so last night,' she observed, dipping into a delightful mixture of chicken and green grapes and walnuts. 'And you look as though you didn't sleep at all.'

'You seem to have an absolute genius for calculating hours, where I'm concerned. And you almost nag me, when it comes to sleep.' Jonathan paused to pick at the food on his plate. 'You see, sleep and I don't get along terribly well. We manage to co-exist most of the time——'

'When you give it the chance,' she put in quickly.

'That's part of it,' he agreed. 'But often it doesn't give me much of a chance.' He pushed his plate aside and Livia saw that he hadn't eaten much at all.

'It looks as though one of you gave the other a pretty bad time of it, last night,' she observed. 'Did you sleep at all?'

'I don't know,' he said with some irritation, worrying the gold medallion with long, slender fingers. 'Am I supposed to keep a log for you?'

Livia shook her head and began clearing away all the stuff of the meal. It seemed a pity, she thought absently, that someone in the hotel had gone to all this trouble for almost nothing. 'What's wrong?' she asked at last.

Jonathan hesitated an instant and then looked away. 'The play. You. Me. It's all not fitting together, somehow—not that my life ever seems to fit together awfully well. But I don't seem to be handling it with my customary flair.' He smiled briefly, mocking himself.

'Perhaps I should have married you on the spot, when you came back from your jungle, all charged up with coffee and jet lag.'

'No.' He shook his head. 'You were right that time. Does it please you to hear me say it?'

'Not as much as I'd expected it would,' she admitted.

'We were both being a bit too righteous that night.' He smiled again, but there wasn't any pleasure in it. 'I don't know what to think now.' And then he corrected himself. 'Well, I do know what to think, but it's not the time. The timing is wrong, now. Does that make any sense to you?'

'Not really. But it doesn't matter.' She reached out and put her hand over his, which was still worrying the medallion. 'Jonathan, you shouldn't let this bother you.' And then, with sudden insight, she continued, 'Perhaps it's that we can't resolve ourselves, until we resolve the play—or am I putting it very badly?'

'Quite well, I think.' Jonathan smiled and took her hand. 'You seem to have gotten a lot older, this last week or so. But I don't think I'm making any sort of equal progress.'

'I don't see how you can be doing anything at all, if you're not getting any sleep. You ought to go back to the hotel—or I'll loan you my couch again, if that would be any help.'

'No.' The idea obviously didn't suit him. 'Let's see if I can handle you and sunlight at the same time.'

'And make idle conversation?' she asked sceptically. 'You aren't fit for idle conversation. At least lie down and close your eyes and stop talking for a while.' And, when he neither moved nor said a word, she leaned forward and placed her hands on his shoulders. 'Look, you've been ordering me around for weeks now—and throwing me around, too, on occasion. Now it's my turn. Just this once, would you please let me tell you what to do?'

She pulled at his shoulders, trying to force him down on to the blanket. She thought, for an instant, that she had caught him off balance. He started to go down and then reached out quickly and caught her by the waist, so that she toppled down under him.

'Jonathan!' she protested, feeling his weight against her, and his face disturbingly close to hers.

'I think you rather asked for that one,' he said with a wicked grin. 'And I'll not complain.' He kissed her soundly and then turned on to his side, taking his weight off her, but pulling her close to him.

Livia felt that she ought to protest, but she really didn't want to. It felt too good—to be so close to him, to feel his breath against her cheek, and to put one hand against his chest and feel his heart beating beneath her touch.

CHAPTER NINE

LIVIA came awake gradually, and it took a while to realise that she was not in her familiar bed. There were strange voices, the sounds of movement not far away, and decidedly hard ground under her. And, she discovered, she could feel the form of someone holding her—Jonathan.

She opened her eyes, blinking against the light, and found his face very near hers. They were, she realised, in something of a tangled heap. He was lying on his side with one arm flung out to create a sort of pillow for them both. His other arm was around her shoulders, holding her firmly in place. Even more surprising was the fact that her free arm was lying across him, her hand resting against the small of his back. Her other hand was where it had been, when she fell asleep—against his chest, feeling the beat of his heart under her fingers.

She thought of the two other times she had watched him sleep, and wondered why he looked so different this time. There were probably a lot of reasons, she decided lazily. She was seeing him in sunlight. And she wasn't looking down at him from a distance, this time. That might explain why his face didn't look so empty, even though he was quite thoroughly asleep. Perhaps a man's face never did look quite so empty, if he slept with someone.

There also seemed to be just a trace of a smile on his lips—that or an elusive, satisfied expression. She couldn't quite put her finger on it, but there seemed to be a measure of content. It was moving, if somewhat frightening, to realise that her presence might be responsible for that content. It seemed enough to simply watch his face, unmindful of the sounds of strangers and the occasional footsteps nearby.

Although she couldn't see it, she judged that the sun was beginning to set. The light was less pure brilliance and more soft gold. The waning sun was also casting shadows, and the planes and angles, the soft shadings of lines, were beginning to come back into his face. Still, she decided with satisfaction, he didn't look quite so bone-weary. She wanted to touch his face, but was afraid that even the slightest movement might wake him.

Perhaps even the thought was enough, because his eyes were suddenly open. 'You've been watching me,' he whispered, smiling crookedly.

'Were you awake all this time?'

'No, but I was, earlier, and I watched you. Now, if you're trying to compute how long I slept, you needn't subtract much, because I was only awake for a few minutes. Just long enough to memorise you, so that you'd still be with me when I went back to sleep again.'

'I think that's an accomplished compliment.'

'No.' His lips brushed hers and then remained against her cheek. 'I'm very good at them when I want to be, but I don't believe I've ever given you anything approaching an accomplished compliment.'

'Then that's the nicest thing of all,' she whispered, and felt his hand stroking her hair, and then working at her scarf until he had pulled it free.

'Now that's something I've wanted to do all day. You're always doing something to hold your hair back. Leave it down for the rest of the day, will you?'

'All right.' At this point she would have done anything he asked.

'We ought to do this more often,' he said with a smile. 'Although I think I'll opt for a bed, next time.'

'You're always willing to opt for a bed,' Livia teased.

'And you're always willing to think the worst of me. You are a shrew, you know. It doesn't matter what I say, you've always got a sharp comeback.'

'You bring out the worst in me,' she explained. 'You're so constantly on the offensive, and I can't seem to resist snapping at you. I can't think why,' she added with a puzzled frown, 'except that you seem to feel that you own the high ground, and I'm determined to prove that you don't. Although I expect you do, actually.'

'What is this high ground you keep talking about?'

'I don't *keep* talking about it,' she corrected. 'It's just an expression that seems to suit you very well.'

'Would it spoil the fun if you told me what it means?'

She shook her head. 'It's a military term—I read about it somewhere. Strategically, one wants to take the high ground. To take control, you see. To win the battle.'

'And that's how you see me?' He asked.

'That's how I see *us*,' She corrected. 'You've got the high ground, and I always seem to be wanting to take it away from you. It's what I said—you bring out the worst in me.'

'Did it ever occur to you that there might be room for both of us on this high ground of yours?'

It seemed to be a serious question, and Livia gave it serious consideration. 'Perhaps. But I can't imagine you willingly sharing the space with anyone who wasn't capable of winning it on his own—or her own, or whatever. Do you follow that?' she asked doubtfully.

'All too well.' Jonathan smiled ruefully. 'It means that I've got to put up with all kinds of barbed comments and provocations from you, until you prove—to your own satisfaction—that you're capable of wresting this high ground away from me.' He sighed, but she knew he was teasing. 'It's going to be a long and wearing battle, isn't it?'

'I expect so,' she agreed with lazy satisfaction. 'But it isn't all a battle. I was rather nice to you this afternoon. You look a great deal better, you know—as though you've really slept for a change. I did do that for you.'

'I suppose you did, although that brings us back to the bed issue again. I'd not be quite so stiff in every joint if I'd had a proper bed. And, as delightful as it is to lie here with you, I think I'd better get up now—while I still can. Besides, we've got to be at Dickon's before too very long, I expect.'

'Why do we have to be at Dickon's?' Livia demanded, pushing herself slightly away. 'Who said anything about Dickon?'

'I did actually, just now. I expect I forgot to mention it to you earlier. He called this morning, to tell me he was having the cast over for a bit of a party tonight.'

'I didn't know anything about it.'

'That's because he called me first, and I told him I'd pass the word on to you.'

'That must have absolutely delighted him—to know that we're on speaking terms outside of rehearsals.' Livia felt uneasy. 'It might have been better if you hadn't said anything. He'd rather we didn't have anything to do with each other. I suppose I'll get another lecture.'

'Livia, will you—just this once—not worry about Dickon, or what he may think of us.'

If she had been uneasy, Jonathan sounded positively irritated. 'Perhaps I won't, any more,' she said almost defiantly, because she had to admit that it was a heady thought. Besides, she wanted to humour Jonathan. 'You may make a loose woman of me yet,' she added for good measure, and then—for a change—she kissed him.

'And you may cause me to permanently dislocate my back, if I don't get up. I've also got a watch somewhere in this tangle we've made of ourselves, and I think I'd better check the time. Otherwise we'll make quite an obviously late entrance at Dickon's.'

'Now who's worrying about what Dickon will say?' she asked sweetly, watching while he unlimbered himself.

'Shrew!' He sat beside her, wincing. 'I'm entirely too old for this sort of activity. And I wasn't worrying about what Dickon might say. I'm not quite sure what I was worrying about—perhaps that Dickon expects people to be on time. Occasionally, much against my will, he does become something of a hair shirt to me.'

'Dickon *is* a hair shirt,' said Livia with some heat, and Jonathan smiled.

'True. But a damned good writer, don't forget that. He's going to make you a star.' And then he grinned wickedly, before getting to his feet and pulling her up after him.

They walked slowly back to Livia's apartment and, without discussion, Jonathan followed her up the stairs.

'You've put me properly through my paces, today, haven't you?' he asked as they reached her door, both slightly breathless.

'What do you mean?' she asked absently, fishing for her key.

'I've climbed these damned stairs twice already, just

for you. Then you made me walk heaven knows how many miles, to get to that river and back. Then—and I rather think this is the crowning injustice—you made me sleep on the ground. Physically, I may never recover.'

'Well, you can go back to your hotel now, and have a nice hot bath.'

'We haven't time for that, Livia darling.' He consulted his watch. 'We're expected at Dickon's in just over half an hour—not that I expect you to be ready that soon. If I go back to the hotel, I'll arrive just in time to turn around and come back for you—and end up doing those seventy-five steps yet again.' He set down the picnic hamper and pulled her close. 'You go change into something interesting—I haven't seen you wear anything interesting since Dickon's last party—while I rest my weary bones on your couch.' He kissed her forehead and then tilted her head up, so that she had to look at him. 'Leave your hair down. It looks quite pagan this way, and I like it.'

And then he kissed her lips, his fingers fanning through her hair, spilling it out against his face.

'You smell like sunshine and green grass,' he whispered, his lips against her hair. 'I just might grow to like sunshine.'

Livia, had she allowed emotion to rule, with no thought of prudence or caution, would willingly have stayed in his arms forever. But Jonathan pushed her away and grinned. 'Lucky for you that Dickon has this party laid on—and that I'm allowing him to be my hair shirt. You'd not be safe, otherwise.'

'I'm not sure I'd want to be,' she answered breathlessly, and he grinned again.

'That's a nice thought, but I think we'd better wait. Now go and get dressed.' He gave her a little push, starting her off down the hall.

'All right,' she called, and shut the bedroom door behind her. It was a bit difficult to concentrate on something as commonplace as dressing, after that brief exchange—after the whole day, for that matter. She had slept in his arms, she thought, staring absently at her reflection in the mirror. She had gone off to sleep feeling the beat of his heart under her fingers; there was enough in that to think about for hours. Still, he had told her to change, and to wear something interesting. And to leave her hair down, she remembered, looking at her reflection with a bit more interest.

Her hair was a tangle, and she set to work, brushing it vigorously until it had a semblance of order. It actually wasn't too bad, she decided, although she had to agree that she did look a bit pagan. Even more to the point was the fact that she didn't look like herself. Livia Paige wore her hair up in a casual knot. She permitted a few strands to stray, but always within a framework of control. 'And isn't that true of your whole life?' she asked herself silently, staring into the mirror. 'Wasn't that Jonathan's point, exactly, the night he asked you to marry him?'

She didn't look at all like the person who had said no, that night—said no because people didn't go and do mad, unplanned things like marrying in haste. Right now, she was forced to admit, she looked like the sort of person who would fall into Jonathan's plans without a moment's hesitation. But that was something that she had better work out some other time. She still had to decide on a dress to wear—something Jonathan would consider interesting.

Nothing in her closet looked interesting. She was sure that she'd once thought her wardrobe interesting, but it seemed that a different Livia had done the selecting. Now everything seemed just a bit too careful, too safe. Certainly nothing was pagan; nothing matched her hair or her mood. The best she was able to do was a casual caftan, a pale pink which deepened into shades of red, with gold patterns through it, around the long hem. The wide and graceful sleeves were the same red and gold pattern, which made for a strange contrast—chaste pink for the bodice, with a nearly pagan effect for the skirt and sleeves.

She hoped it would be interesting enough for Jonathan, even though it wasn't quite as abandoned a dress as she might have liked to have. She slipped on a pair of red leather shoes, almost ballet slippers. They had no heels at all, which would put her at a greater height disadvantage than usual, but they were the only shoes she had to match. Then, with one final look in the mirror and a defiant toss of her head, she left the bedroom.

Jonathan was studying her books, when she came into the living room. He was bent over, fingering titles on one of the lower shelves, the gold medallion swinging and catching a bit of the setting sun through her window. He looked up as she entered the room and eyed her appreciatively.

'That's a bit more like it.' He nodded approval. 'You'll have to wear your hair up in the play, but I like it this way. Of course, in the play, I'm not supposed to like you, am I?'

'I expect not,' she agreed, feeling suddenly shy.

'And you certainly aren't about to do anything to please me, in the play. I don't find any grammar books among your collection,' he observed, with one of his sudden shifts.

'Why should you?' she asked blankly.

'Because you're so good at pronouns. I thought you might spend your evenings studying up on them—

when no one was looking—but you must come by it naturally.'

'They're a family conceit,' she explained. 'We rather like to be different, and using pronouns properly is one way of being different, where I grew up, if you can believe such a thing.'

'Oh, I expect I can believe almost anything about your family and your town.' Jonathan smiled. 'I have my conceits, too, although none of them are family ones. Difficult to manage when one hasn't a family, and I haven't. This is one of them,' he added, in a sudden shift which seemed to Livia to have the purpose of getting away from his lack of family. He pulled the medallion off over his head, and handed it to her.

The edges were somewhat irregular, and it was well worn, but Livia could make out that it was a coin of some sort, and a very old one at that. On one side there was a man's profile, and she thought she could see the remains of a wreath around the head. 'Is it Roman?' she asked doubtfully. 'One of the Caesars?'

'Julius, in fact.' He seemed pleased that she'd been correct. 'I played Julius Caesar, back in prep school. I expect every actor has one part from years ago—one that told him this was it, this was what he must do with his life. Caesar was mine. That's why I wear this.'

'And you've never done it professionally, have you?' Livia asked.

'Not yet. I expect I shall, some day.' He paused to smile lazily. Although I now think I'd rather play Augustus Caesar, if there were a part worth doing.'

'Why?' she asked, sensing a hidden meaning she didn't understand.

'Oh, a variety of reasons. He's an interesting character, with an interesting life. You ought to read up on him some time.'

'And that's all the help I'm going to get?'

'That's right. You'll have to do your homework.'

'But I explained the high ground to you,' she protested.

'So you did,' he agreed thoughtfully. 'Why not?' He appeared almost ill at ease. 'Augustus was married to Livia—at least at one point. I expect he was married more than once, though. All the Caesars seem to have been. We'd better go now,' he hurried on. 'We're late as it is.'

'Right,' said Livia carefully, trying not to make too much of what he had just said. She handed him back the coin on the chain.

He took it, fingered it for a moment, and then spread the chain open and slipped it over her head. 'You wear it. It suits your dress, and it is quite pagan, you know.'

'But I can't!' she protested. 'It's yours. You were wearing it, and it does look quite spectacular.'

'No.' Jonathan reached out one hand, to free her hair where it was caught under the chain. 'It's yours now.' He flashed the wicked grin. 'If you'd allowed yourself to get to know me considerably better, you'd have found that I always wear it. But it's always under my shirt. I can't think why I left it out, today. It's always seemed to me that I'm quite flamboyant enough, without adding to the effect. You, on the other hand—' he studied her quizzically—'you need all the help you can get.'

There were a number of tart responses to that comment, but Livia realised that none of them would be exactly truthful. She probably did need all the help she could get.

'No argument,' said Jonathan in wonder. 'Livia caught with nothing to say! But now we're off to Dickon's, and I'll go into my act, and you'll find plenty to say—all of it bad, if the last party is anything to go by.'

'I didn't say anything critical last time,' she protested.

'Not out loud, that's true. But you say things so eloquently, without ever saying a word. I've told you that before.'

'Yes,' she agreed, starting for the door. 'But I'm not quite as predictable as you may think.'

'That sounds rather promising.' Jonathan grinned again and they started down the stairs.

It was the second time Livia had made a late entrance at one of Dickon's parties, but this time was very different. The last time she had arrived with Perry. Jonathan had been dominating a full house, and only Dickon had noticed her arrival. This time the room appeared as full, but there was no real focal point. People stood about in aimless little groups and there was a well defined waiting quality in the air.

'We're late, but we're here!' Jonathan called, striding into the room as it suddenly came alive. He had Livia by the hand, and she felt like a reluctant child being dragged into a room full of strangers. Bright dress, pagan hair, golden chain and coin notwithstanding, she was definitely eclipsed by the larger than life presence of Jonathan.

They were immediately surrounded by the others, although Livia had to concede that only Jonathan would have been had he not continued to hold her hand. He was already off on a story, but Livia wasn't listening. She was studying the faces in the group around them—the open admiration and sudden sense of wellbeing reflected by them all.

Then she felt a light touch on her shoulder and turned to find Dickon beside her. 'May I talk to you for a minute?' he asked softly. 'There are a couple of things I need to say.'

'I'm sure there are,' she said tartly, and turned back to Jonathan long enough to disengage her hand. He didn't appear to even notice.

When she was free, Dickon took her gently by the arm and led her across the room to the windows. 'I didn't know you were seeing Jonathan today,' he began.

'I didn't either, until he woke me out of a sound sleep to tell me that we were going on a picnic.'

'Is that all you did?' Dickon asked with evident relief.

'That's right,' she said steadily. 'What's the matter? Did you think we were going to spend the day in my bed or his?' And then, seeing the shocked expression on his face, she added, 'You're worse than my mother, you know. She doesn't check up on me constantly.'

'Perhaps she doesn't realise the danger you're in.'

'Oh, Dickon,' she sighed, 'don't talk such rubbish!' She fingered the Roman coin, wishing she had a drink, something to occupy her hands.

Dickon caught the movement of her hand and stared at the coin for a moment. 'I've seen that, haven't I?' he asked, his voice heavy with significance.

'I wouldn't know.' Livia shrugged and wondered what was possessing her. 'It depends on how well you know Jonathan.'

'That's what I thought.' It was his turn to sigh. 'Livy, I don't think you know what you're getting into.' And seeing her about to protest, he hurried on, 'I'm sorry—I know you wish I wouldn't say these things, but I think you must understand my feelings, too. There was a time, perhaps a year or so ago, when I thought we might grow to care for one another.'

He paused uncertainly, to gauge her reaction, but he

had left her speechless. This particular development had never entered her head. Finding no objection, he continued, 'But I'm a realist. I'm living the sort of life that suits me. It's pleasant and comfortable, but not terribly glamorous. It's a very settled sort of life, and I have the feeling that your life—with or without Jonathan—is about to become most unsettled.' He regarded her dress, as though the combination of pink, red and gold already indicated a certain degree of unsettledness. 'And so'—he sighed, a bit regretfully, she thought—'I realise that there isn't any future for us. Your life is going to be quite different, and we simply wouldn't be compatible. But, because of this feeling I've had, you must understand if I worry about you.'

And what on earth does one say to that? Livia wondered wildly. Her first impulse was to tell him that, for a playwright who used tight and brief dialogue, he certainly ran on and repeated himself in his real life. But that wouldn't do at all. 'Dickon,' she began slowly, playing for time, 'you're very kind, and I know that you mean well. But I don't think you've ever known me as well as you think you do. It's not just that my life may become quite different—with or without Jonathan, as you put it. It always has been quite different. It's just that the difference didn't show, before. And perhaps even I didn't see it very clearly. But we've never had much in common, except a good friendship. And you really mustn't presume to tell me what to do, or to give me any warnings—any more than I would presume to do the same to you.'

'I see,' he said coolly. 'I stand corrected.'

'Oh, don't get all stuffy about this!' Livia glanced away and saw that Jonathan was still holding court, apparently oblivious to the fact that she was trapped with Dickon and a difficult situation. 'We're still good friends,' she added, and hated herself for the triteness. Still, Dickon himself was rather trite, except in his writing. 'And good friends needn't agree on every thing.' She patted his hand casually and started to turn away. 'I really think we've said it all, don't you?' She was eager to be away and, for once, Dickon seemed to have read her correctly.

'Yes, we have. And you have other places to go, haven't you?'

She nodded and then smiled at him, a friendly, forgiving smile, before walking away. She stopped just outside the group around Jonathan and began to watch him with a steady stare. Sooner or later he would look up and see her, although she wasn't quite sure what she would do when he did.

It didn't take him long. He turned slightly, apparently to catch what someone in the group was saying, and his eyes met hers. 'Here's Livia,' he said loudly. 'And looking quite disapproving, too. I must have done something wrong.'

'Not at all,' she called back across the space between them. 'I'm only watching you.' Heads turned in her direction for the first time. 'You see,' she said, addressing the others, 'I must loathe him as a character. And, as a director, I frequently do—quite sincerely. He is a bit of a tyrant, don't you think?' Her eyes challenged the others, and there was a ripple of nervous laughter. 'I thought it might be instructive to see if he has any redeeming qualities, when he's being neither character nor director.' She looked up at Jonathan, pleased that she had, at least for the moment, taken the centre stage away from him. In his eyes she saw a glint of surprise, and he was smiling, as though she had pleased him.

'But I thought I'd already proved that,' he protested. 'I took her on a picnic today, and I consider that a rather decent thing to do. I didn't snap at her once.'

'No. How could you?' she shot back. 'You fell asleep!'

'Unfair,' he murmured. 'You'll ruin my image.'

'I doubt it. It would take more than my feeble efforts.'

'They're not feeble, Livia—they're quite considerable. More than I'd expected, actually.' That last appeared to be directed only at her, without thought for the audience hanging on every word. And then he was back in character again, playing to everyone. 'I expect I'd better charm her for a while, or she'll turn shrew on me.' He moved through the group and draped one arm casually over her shoulders. 'I'm not quite so bad, am I?'

'I haven't decided yet. You'll have to stay awake long enough to give me a reasonable sample of your better qualities—if you have any,' she added as a deliberate afterthought.

He turned her away from the group and bent down to whisper in her ear, 'Do you mind telling me what's got into you?'

'What's wrong?' she asked sweetly, not bothering to lower her voice. 'Does it bother you that I took the spotlight away?'

'You know perfectly well it's not that,' he drawled, and went through the clumsy process of lighting a cigarette with only one hand, keeping the other firmly around her.

'You wanted me to be pagan, and I'm doing the best I can. Besides, I'm harbouring a grudge right now. You must have seen that Dickon had me trapped for a great length of time. You might have done something to rescue me.'

'I saw all that. I don't miss much, you know. But I

rather thought you'd have to settle that one for yourself. He was proposing, wasn't he?'

'No, you got that wrong. He was just nattering on about us again. And you might have told me,' she added with venom, 'that he'd recognise the coin you gave me to wear. That's what set him off in the first place.'

'Never gave it a thought,' Jonathan said blandly.

'Well, I wish you had!' she snapped. 'You can't imagine how disconcerting it is to have someone telling you that you ought not get involved with someone else, and that he's only telling you because he'd have gotten involved with you himself, except that you're already involved, or going on to greater things, or something of the sort. All in the middle of a party—grant you, no one could possibly be listening, because they were all listening to the person you're supposed to be involved with.'

'Livia dear——' he kissed her cheek with a florish she was sure did not go unnoticed—'you're making no sense at all.'

'I'm sure I'm not. It's also disconcerting to be trying to explain all this—also in the middle of a party—where everyone is listening, or trying to.'

'Which they wouldn't be able to do, if you'd keep your voice down,' Jonathan pointed out reasonably. 'I think I'd better get you a drink, if you'll promise to behave yourself during the few minutes I'm gone. And you needn't worry about other people hearing what you just said. Even if they did, they won't understand it any better than I did.'

He turned away and began moving slowly through the group—wicked grin and all, Livia noted, as she watched him exchange comments with first one and then another.

'Have you and Jonathan had a fight or something?'

Livia turned to find Perry by her side, looking interested and somewhat concerned.

'I'm not sure,' Livia answered absently. She was suddenly aware of Dickon, still standing by the windows, looking suitably reproachful.

'I'm not, either.' Perry seemed to be mulling things over. 'Something very strange does seem to be going on, though.'

'Something very strange is always going on when Jonathan is around,' Livia snapped, but Perry shook his head.

'No, it's not just Jonathan. It's you, too, Livy. First you huddle with Dickon and completely ignore the rest of us, and then you come over and get very stagey, which isn't like you, normally. Perhaps you're beginning to feel like a star,' he suggested brightly.

'Hardly that. I think I'm in over my head, right now.'

'She isn't, you know,' Jonathan remarked casually, materialising beside them, but picking up the thread of conversation as though he'd been there the whole time. 'She may think she is, but it's quite the reverse, actually.' He handed Livia a drink and smiled appreciatively at her.

Perry appeared to give that comment considerable thought and Livia realised that he had also caught Jonathan's smile. 'Oh. Rising to the occasion, or something like that?' he asked.

'Something like that,' Jonathan agreed.

Perry took another moment to mull that one over, glancing from Jonathan to Livia and back again. Then he smiled brightly, as though he'd suddenly worked things through in his mind. 'Well,' he said casually, 'I expect I ought to get a drink, or talk to someone, or something.' He slipped away.

Jonathan watched his retreat with a tolerant smile.

'He might just as well have suggested that the two of us would like to be alone. I expect that was the best he could do at being subtle.'

'At least *he* didn't give us a lecture. I couldn't stand another one.' She took a quick sip of her drink and discovered that Jonathan had given her straight Scotch—not, perhaps, the wisest thing on an empty stomach.

'You're having a bad night,' Jonathan observed with absolutely no trace of sympathy.

'I know,' she sighed. 'I do wish Dickon would stop.'

At that moment the stereo began blasting, effectively drowning out conversation. Jonathan put his hand on her arm and steered her into a far corner of the room.

'That's better,' he said approvingly. 'That will give us the privacy we ought to have, whether you think so or not.'

Livia took a second, cautious, sip of her drink. 'You know, for someone who's such an old and supposedly good friend, Dickon doesn't seem to think much of you.'

'Read the play and you'll find that he doesn't think much of you, either,' Jonathan pointed out.

'I hadn't thought of that.'

'Of course you hadn't. You're much too nice. You don't expect people to be devious, or to do hateful things to others.'

'Is that bad?' she asked doubtfully. 'To be nice, I mean.'

'Don't be silly.' He smiled at her with tender amusement. 'Most of us ought to worry because we're not nice enough, and here you are, trying to be nice to everyone—completely missing the fact that not everyone is trying to be nice to you. I rather like it, and I can't imagine how you retain the quality, working in a business like this.'

'Perhaps it comes of trying to avoid success—
creeping back to Boston, where I don't have to make
any decisions,' she said with sudden daring, throwing
back at him his own words from that hurtful night.

'Let's not get into all that,' he said uncomfortably.
'I know it sounds trite to tell you that I said a lot of
things I didn't really mean, that night. But I did.' He
smiled, a crooked, almost apologetic smile. 'You see, I
thought it quite remarkable that I was prepared to
actually marry someone. Quite out of character and
rather revolutionary of me. It stung to find that you
weren't as appreciative of my gesture as I thought you
ought to be.'

'I was appreciative of the gesture,' she said
seriously. 'I just didn't think we ought to jump into it
quite so abruptly.'

'I know. That's your stability, or your sanity—
whatever it is. And I ought to have been more
forgiving, because what made you say no was the
quality I liked best about you.'

'I'm not sure how I feel about all those past tenses,'
she said quickly, and then wished she hadn't.

'Don't worry about tenses.' He pulled her close and
kissed her briefly.

'They're going to be looking,' Livia whispered
uncomfortably.

'That doesn't matter.' He circled her with one arm,
so that she couldn't move. 'This is what they expect of
me. I'm supposed to get some girl off in a corner and
flirt outrageously. Anyway, I told them that I had to
charm you for a while. Now I'm obviously succeeding,
which is rather obliging of you—preserving my
reputation and all that.'

'Now you're not being serious.'

'Of course I am. I'm just telling you how the others
will see this.' He grinned. 'We can be just as

affectionate as we please, and no one will think a thing
of it—except to see that I haven't lost my touch.' Then
he looked at her quite seriously, tracing the line of her
face with one finger. 'I've never been as close to
anyone as I have been to you, today. Don't let it stop
now, just because people happen to be watching.'

There was no arguing with that, Livia realised. It
was a rather significant admission from someone like
Jonathan. It made her love him even more.

After that, Livia behaved rather outrageously herself—
at least by her own standards. With Jonathan beside
her, and given all that had passed between them, it
suddenly seemed the only way to behave. It was a
heady sensation to be quite so open about how she felt,
to allow him to keep his arm around her, and to return
his kisses without restraint. But the greatest of her
delights was simply to watch him, to see the animation
in his face as he talked to her or to others. She
memorised his features, watched the way one lock of
hair fell across his forehead and the movement of his
hand as he occasionally brushed it back.

She wondered if he had ever watched her in the
same way. Through all those weeks when she had been
afraid to be free and open, had he been watching her
in the way she now watched him? She hoped he had,
although he certainly hadn't been as obvious about it
as she was being.

And it was that obviousness which finally brought
the evening to an end for her. At last Jonathan pulled
her aside, studying her face.

'You ought to go home,' he told her.

'Just me?' she asked with daring.

He nodded. 'Just you. I'm good until dawn, but I
think you're not. Anyway, I wouldn't be responsible
for my actions, if I took you home.'

'You wouldn't need to be.'

He grinned. 'That's the problem, love. I don't think it's going to help the play, if we begin to feel too comfortable about one another.'

'I don't care about the damn play,' she said mutinously.

'You'd better, by Monday morning. That's why you're going home now, and alone. And I won't see you again until rehearsal—by which time you'd better be back to normal.'

'I don't know what you mean.'

'I mean that you've got to behave quite differently than you have tonight. Self-indulgence time is over. No more love in your eyes, no charming capitulation— none of that.' He kissed her gently and then let her go. 'My driver is outside; he'll take you home.'

'Your driver!' she mocked, feeling more than a little like Cinderella at midnight—even if it was well past midnight. 'I can walk.'

'You're not walking home, at this time of night. And you're not going to spoil the play by walking through it with your heart in your eyes.'

'Then you shouldn't have been so nice. You shouldn't have encouraged me,' she objected sadly.

'Perhaps I shouldn't,' Jonathan agreed without remorse, and walked her to the door.

CHAPTER TEN

LIVIA arrived at the theatre with the best of intentions. She understood what Jonathan meant: she couldn't allow her feelings for him to colour her performance. The whole thrust of her character would be to feel the reverse of everything she actually felt for Jonathan now. As he had said, 'Self-indulgence time is over.'

But that was easier to know than to accomplish. Livia arrived early at the theatre, and it seemed an age until she heard Jonathan's voice. Seeing him again was like seeing him for the first time. He was tall and lean, showing an incredible energy. He couldn't wait to start work, she realised. The play was all coming together for him. The nerves and tensions of the past, when he had been displeased with things, were gone. Things were pretty well locked into place, with just two more days for refinements. Then came the dress rehearsal, and then the opening, on Thursday. Livia sensed that refinements were what Jonathan liked best. Laying down the part and finding character was hard work; everyone struggled with those tasks. What set Jonathan apart from any other actor with whom she had ever worked was the effort he made to add shadings and brief flashes to basic work. She sensed that he was relishing that process. He couldn't wait to start the day's work.

'Last act, last scene!' he called, not appearing particularly interested in the fact that Livia was present. Except, she decided, for the fact that he couldn't *do* the last act, last scene, without her.

'There are a few things I haven't got right,' he

explained. 'Livia, I'm afraid you're going to have to bear with me, until I manage to please myself.'

'Which won't be easy, I expect.' She smiled, but he didn't seem to notice, so she took her place and waited for him to begin.

He'd been giving the scene a lot of thought, she realised immediately. There were subtle changes—gestures and variations of expression which hadn't been there before. It was a marvel to watch—the difference between a good actor and a great one. There was nothing obvious about what he was doing, nothing she could really identify. But the sum of the parts was going to make for a memorable performance. And she found that his new ideas stimulated her to try things of her own, things which must have been waiting, just outside conscious thought. They had never played it quite so well, she decided, as they approached the very end.

This was the moment when she must not hear him at all, and that hadn't been an easy trick to master. She had to be listening at the start, and Jonathan had allowed her the freedom to decide when she would mentally depart. She had, some time before, settled on a point about a third of the way through his speech. She had managed—after many false starts—to achieve a true inability to hear a word he said. It was, as he had once told her, one thing to act like a character who isn't hearing what is being said, and quite another to *be* a person who doesn't hear a thing.

She'd had it down, but she suddenly seemed unable to make it happen. The problem was a combination of two new developments. The first was that Jonathan was doing exciting new things with his lines, and she wanted to hear and see what he was doing. The second was, of course, that they had shared so much, just two days before; it made it impossible not to want to hear him and be aware of everything about him.

Livia knew that she wasn't getting her part right; she didn't think that he was aware of her difficulty. He was working too hard on his own part, she believed. It wasn't until he was completely done that she realised she had misjudged him.

'Damn it, you heard that!' He turned on her the instant he'd said his last words.

'Well, only this time. I was interested to see what you'd done with it,' she explained, and didn't add that she'd also slept in his arms, his heart beating beneath her fingers.

'We open in two days,' he said with icy control. 'You can't be hearing it one time and not the next. We haven't time to start over.'

'We won't need to start over,' she assured him.

He gave her a sceptical glance. 'Then lay my fears at rest by going through it again.'

And so they did it again, but this time Livia was too conscious of his attention to her, and his doubts. She did better, but it still wasn't right. His voice kept intruding, no matter how hard she tried to keep it out. When they were done, he merely shook his head.

'Again,' he commanded.

Livia took a steadying breath and they started in again. But it wasn't getting any better; it was getting worse. She had too much self-awareness, and he wasn't handling her properly. If he would take her aside and let her discuss it with him calmly, she would be able to get it back, she thought resentfully. Instead, he was badgering her and showing no understanding at all.

When they finished the third try, Jonathan was silent for a few minutes, his back to her. Then he turned and started with deceptive calmness. 'Yes. Well, you said you'd heard me, but that it was only going to be for that one time. Now you've heard me for the third time. You don't seem to be able to be very professional about this, do you, Livia?'

'I'm trying,' she said ineffectually.

'But not succeeding. Perhaps you need more of the play, to get yourself into character. So we will——' and here he raised his voice, so that the other members of the cast would know with certainty that they were included—'start from the beginning. We have to do it some time, anyway. It will also give me a chance to see if you've lost any more of it,' he added, to Livia alone.

They started from the beginning, Livia feeling almost weary, although it was still early in the day. She wasn't getting any of it right, she realised. She was coming close some of the time, and there were brief moments when she hit her stride again. But most of it was wrong, and it rang hollow in her ears.

Jonathan had been quite right. She was going to spoil the play, if she walked through it with her heart in her eyes. But he had been wrong to think it would be enough to send her home alone from the party. He should never have spent the day with her. He shouldn't have let himself get so close to her—not just physically close, but emotionally. *He* could let himself get that close and then, through sheer force of will or greater talent, put it behind him. She could not. She wanted to blame him. He had put her in a position where she had to handle how much she loved him, and still do the play as it ought to be done. But it wasn't his fault; it was her own lack of ability. She couldn't separate them, as people who loved each other, from the characters.

Jonathan knew it, too, and he stopped them before they were halfway through the first act.

'Something rather interesting has happened here,' he began mildly, addressing not only Livia but the others as well. 'It's vital that Livia have her part right.

I don't mean to slight the rest of you, but this is, basically, a two-person play.' He paused to light a cigarette and began pacing. 'As you may have noticed, Livia suddenly doesn't have her part right. Last week she was doing a terrific job. Today, it's gone. You may be wondering why. I don't need to wonder, nor does Livia. We know, don't we?' He looked enquiringly at her, but she couldn't speak. She knew, at least in part, what was coming.

'I made an error in judgment this weekend. I took Livia on a picnic, which seemed harmless enough. And then, as you all heard, I fell asleep. What Livia didn't tell you was that I fell asleep in her arms, and she in mine.'

No, Livia protested silently, don't tell it all. Don't make it shabby and adolescent. She drew a ragged breath, and it echoed hollowly on the silent stage. Jonathan shot her a brief, unfeeling look.

'She'd rather I didn't say all this. She'd rather keep it our little secret—even though it's all over the stage, for anyone with half a brain to see. But I'm going to explain it, because you've all worked hard enough to deserve an explanation.

'It was what one might call a romantic interlude. Perhaps we—each of us—made more of it than we ought to have. You all saw the results at Dickon's party. We couldn't keep our hands, or our eyes, off one another. It was also a miscalculation—a mistake—on my part. I may be able to do a play like this and handle emotional involvement at the same time. Livia apparently cannot. Perhaps it's easier for me, because I know that it really didn't mean a thing.'

Not true! Livia told herself. We both know how much it meant, how much it does mean.

'And,' he continued, 'having done the damage, I have now got to try to find a way to undo it. Livia may think she cares more about me than she does about this play, but I care only about the play. And I'll be damned if I'll let her ruin it for all of us.' By this time his face was white with controlled anger, and a pulse was beating furiously at his temple.

'Now, the rest of you can break for lunch, whether it's time or not. I want the theatre cleared—no one here except Livia. And while you're gone, she and I will try to settle this.'

He made a sweeping gesture of dismissal and, without a word or a look in Livia's direction, everyone left. She stood, rooted to the spot, hearing the hollow sound of footsteps, cut off suddenly by the closing of the stage door.

For a moment Jonathan said nothing. He seemed to waver indecisively; then, with sudden resolution, he turned to face her.

'Have I made the issue clear?' he asked.

'I think so,' she answered, wishing her voice would not shake.

'I could have made it much clearer, you know. You may not like what I had to say, but it's the truth.'

She started to protest, but he cut her off.

'It is not, however, the whole truth, and you ought to be grateful that I didn't humiliate you further by going into the rest of it.'

'I'm not sure what you mean,' she said unsteadily.

'I could have told them how big a fool I've been,' he continued bitterly. 'I could have explained that I went so far one night as to ask you to marry me, and you turned me down.'

'That doesn't have anything to do with it,' Livia said miserably.

'Oh yes, it does. I thought I loved you—thought you loved me—even after that slap in the face. And we made another try, didn't we? Quite a successful one, too, by the look of things. Oh, yes! By Saturday night I was sure I loved you. And then you did this to me. Out of love?

'I live here, on the stage. This is my life—the only life I have, the only life that never lets me down. I was prepared to let you be a part of that life, but you don't care, do you? I told you that the time for self-indulgence was over, but you don't care. You'd rather have your rosy little romance, and damn the play, or my needs, or anything except what *you* want.

'I might have explained all that to the others, but I thought I ought to salvage some of your pride. But that's all I am going to salvage. I'm not going to let you keep your rosy little romance, because it doesn't exist now. There's nothing here any more, Livia.' He made a sweeping gesture, bringing one hand up against his chest. 'There's no second chance—do you understand that? It's over.' He spaced the words with bitter venom and then stopped, brooding off into space. 'Now perhaps, with that in mind, you can shake off all those romantic little thoughts you've been having about me. Just possibly you can make this play work. But it's quite immaterial to me at this point. Is that understood?'

Livia nodded, not daring to trust her voice.

'And there's just one more point—a small one, but it matters to me. Could you possibly get that Roman coin back to me? It was a loan, not a gift.'

Her humiliation might as well be complete, she decided numbly. There was no point in pretending that she wasn't wearing it under her dress. Her hands were shaking as she drew it out and took it off. She held it for just a moment, cradling it in the palm of her hand, prepared to hand it to him.

'How very touching,' he said with malice. 'Wearing

it near your heart, perhaps? You ought to have got that sort of thing our of your system years ago.'

That was the final blow, but it didn't cause Livia to crumble. Instead she felt a fierce surge of emotion, an almost overwhelming fury. She pulled back her hand, made a fist, and then threw the medallion as hard as she could, straight at him.

As soon as she had done that, she turned and started for the door. She heard the sound of metal hitting the floor, and then Jonathan's voice, sounding both cold and uninterested.

'Do you plan to come back?'

'I haven't decided!' she yelled with a wonderful feeling of release, and slammed the stage door behind her.

She knew where the others were most likely to go for lunch, so she deliberately set out in the opposite direction. Walking helped. Brushing furiously past others, ignoring their looks of surprise, she kept walking until she reached the Public Garden. There she found an empty bench and sat down abruptly, because she realised she was shaking too much to keep going.

She knew that there wasn't time to go into everything Jonathan had said. She had one decision to make, and she had to make it in a hurry. She had to decide if she would go back, if she could go back. If she did, she'd have to do the play right—although that didn't seem to be any great problem now. She wouldn't have her heart in her eyes this time. And if she didn't go back, she'd never be able to act again.

It was like falling off a horse, she decided. You either got right back on, or you never rode again. Never having fallen from a horse, she couldn't be sure if that were true. But she did know that she could never face anyone connected with the theatre, if she didn't go back to this play and do it right.

Well, she wanted the theatre. She'd thought she wanted Jonathan, but that was a dead issue. The theatre wasn't. Strange, she thought, how easy it was to make that decision. Jonathan might have savaged her—in fact he had—but he hadn't destroyed her. There was some consolation to be found in that fact.

She sat on the bench for a few more minutes, breathing fresh air, lifting her face to the cool breeze. She was going back; she knew that now. She'd go back, and she'd do the job properly. It didn't matter if she took her time in returning. She was entitled to a little temperament, wasn't she? But even that thought began to seem less than worthy, so she got up from the bench and started back.

She walked slowly this time, so it took her considerably longer to return to the theatre. As she turned the corner and started down the alley, she could see Perry and Honey just entering the building. That suggested that the whole dreadful business hadn't taken as long as she'd thought. Apparently one could experience a great many profound changes in an hour's time. One could, for example, learn that the man one thought one loved was not at all what he seemed to be. Unprincipled, ruthless, uncaring, capricious—it really didn't matter. One could find that one's love affair was over—if, indeed, it had ever been real. And then, after all that, one could make a momentous and rather courageous decision about the future of one's life—all in the space of one hour. She felt the beginnings of hysteria, as she contemplated what had happened to her in the last hour. But there wasn't any time for hysteria. Now was the time for cold passion, if such a thing existed. To Livia, it appeared that it did, because she seemed to have an abundance of it.

She walked on to the stage just behind Perry and Honey, and they turned to stare. Perry looked really anxious, really concerned. Honey was frankly curious. Livia smiled briefly. Before she could think of anything to say, she heard Jonathan's voice from the auditorium.

'I was wondering when, or if, you'd come back.' His voice sounded very cool, very casual, and there was just a hint of sarcasm in it.

Livia looked out across the stage and found him in the dim light. He was sitting about four rows back, legs stretched out into the aisle. One arm was draped casually across the back of the next seat, and he appeared to be completely at ease.

'I didn't want to leave you in suspense for too long,' she answered, hoping she sounded as cool as she felt. 'I thought I might be allowed to indulge in a little temperament, but not too awfully much. Your point was that I ought to be more professional, wasn't it?'

He stood up. 'That's one way of putting it, I suppose. Are you ready to start?'

'More than ready.'

'Fine.' Jonathan came slowly up the aisle. 'Since the others aren't back yet, with the exception of our two young friends here, we'll start with that last scene again. I'll see if you can get it right this time.'

Livia knew that she could get it right. She could do it exactly as Dickon intended the woman to do it. She could do it better than Jonathan had ever thought she could. It wasn't even acting, any more. Before Jonathan was even up on the stage, she had taken her place and was waiting for him.

Vaguely, in some other part of her mind, Livia was aware of cast members returning, as she and Jonathan went through the last scene. But she was not aware of Jonathan, not when she reached the point where she was not supposed to hear him. She had left the stage and retreated into some dark corner, where nothing could reach her. However, there was no sense of accomplishment, once the scene was over. It didn't matter, not even when Jonathan nodded his approval.

'It would appear,' he began, addressing the cast at large, 'that my lecture has had some effect; Livia's getting it right now. Battles of will can get pretty intense in the theatre, but they are sometimes necessary. If you hadn't already learned that, then perhaps today's little episode provided a good object lesson. Wouldn't you agree, Livia?' he asked, turning to her, his face totally devoid of emotion.

'Yes,' she agreed evenly, striving for the same sense of emptiness which seemed easy for him to achieve.

'I thought so.' She smiled briefly, but it wasn't a pleasant smile. 'Livia's learned quite a few lessons today, I should think. So have I, for that matter.' He was silent for a moment. 'And that's all to the good, I expect.' Then he smiled again, a cold and wintry smile, before he called for the next scene.

CHAPTER ELEVEN

Livia greeted the timid knock at the door with all the fervour of a drowning victim reaching for a lifeline. No matter that her policy had always been to be left alone on the days of openings. That policy seemed not to be working well at all; she needed company—any company—rather badly.

It was Maureen, looking more tentative than Livia had ever seen her.

'If you don't want me, just say so,' Maureen began doubtfully. 'I just wondered how you were.'

'Absolutely thrilled to see you,' Livia said with considerable passion, and then drew a shaky breath. 'I've tried a long hot bath, and I've tried cleaning the apartment, and I've done my nails, and—just before you came—I'd started to just sit, to see if being absolutely still might help. I didn't expect it to, though. Nothing else has.'

'Is it as bad as that?' Maureen asked with sympathy.

'Worse. I feel like a block of ice that isn't melting—at least I think I do. It's hard to say.' And then, realizing that Maureen was still standing in the open doorway, Livia belatedly remembered that she had some obligations as a hostess. 'Come in,' she urged.

'If you're sure?'

'Of course I'm sure. I couldn't be more sure.' She watched Maureen settle herself in her accustomed spot on the couch. 'I'm not handling this very well, you see. I've always found it best to be alone before a play opens, but it seems to have been a very bad idea this time. Of course, this time is awfully different.'

'This time the play is important to your career,' Maureen supplied helpfully.

'Yes,' Livia agreed thoughtlessly, and then sobered. It wasn't just the play, of course. It was trying to handle all the feelings of the play while trying to avoid all the feelings about Jonathan.

'You look as though you'd just seen a ghost,' Maureen said almost gently, studying Livia's face.

'Perhaps I did.' The ghost of what might have been, she added mentally. But I absolutely can't think about that now. 'What time is it?' she asked abruptly.

'About four. I came home early, because *I* couldn't stand the suspense.' Maureen laughed selfconsciously. 'I couldn't stay at work, thinking about you opening in something important—all that it's going to mean to you.'

'You're awfully good,' said Livia in a sudden rush of gratitude.

'Well, it isn't every day that I get exposed to something like this,' Maureen grinned, casting off the air of one visiting a gravely ill friend. 'And I'll get to see Jonathan Worth tonight, not just you. Although I expect to see more of him, now that you've got all this business of rehearsing and battling out of the way. You will introduce me some time, won't you?'

Livia could only stare at Maureen blankly, making no sense of the words. Words about Jonathan—normal, happy words—made no sense at all.

'When you start your affair,' Maureen explained with an impish smile. 'Or, if you're going to keep on being a *good* girl, when you start a grand but chaste romance.'

'There isn't going to be anything like that,' Livia said in a stricken voice. And then, because she couldn't help herself, because she had to say something to someone, she continued, 'I ruined it all—at least I think I did. I'm not sure, though, because I'm not sure it ever could have worked. I'm not sure he's capable of that—some people aren't, and I think perhaps he's one of them.'

'What are you talking about?' Maureen asked softly, seeing Livia's obvious distress.

'Jonathan.' And then, about to explain it all, Livia realised that she couldn't, that she absolutely could not start in on all that—not at this point. 'Later,' she said. 'I'll tell you later.'

'All right,' Maureen agreed, her face grave. 'Can I do anything for you?'

'No, but maybe you would stay while I get dressed?'

'You've got more than three hours,' Maureen pointed out logically.

'I know, but I always have to be early. Being backstage is steadying, somehow. It's the right place for panic, so the panic doesn't seem so bad.' And then, because she had the feeling that she might run on endlessly, if she didn't stop now, Livia retreated down the hall.

When she came back a few minutes later, Maureen was standing in the doorway, holding something in her hand.

'Look what you've just got!' she began. 'A young man just knocked at the door and said this was for you.' She held out a single gardenia, milky white against its dark green leaves. 'He wouldn't even let me tip him, said it was taken care of.'

'Is there a card?' Livia asked, taking the flower.

'I don't see one.'

Livia studied the little flower, puzzled. It was a simple white gardenia, the sort flower sellers have outside the theatre doors before performances. Nothing in the least remarkable about it. Except—she caught her breath and smiled.

'What is it?' Maureen prompted.

'Something awfully nice. It's from my mother, I know it is, although I can't think how she managed to find one before six in the evening, or who she found to deliver it. You see, I was fourteen the first time I ever saw a real professional play. We came down to Boston, just the two of us, to go shopping, and we went to the theatre one night.' She smiled reminiscently.

'You can't imagine how grand it was—I'd never seen anything so grand or so right. I just knew, right on the spot, that I wanted to be part of that world. And I told my mother, also right on the spot, and she didn't laugh, and she made me believe that I might just do it, if I wanted it badly enough. We still talk about that night sometimes, and she always calls it the night that changed my life—which it did, of course.'

'But what does that have to do with a gardenia?' Maureen asked blankly.

'She bought me one that night. There was a flower seller outside the theatre, and she told me that gardenias were a sort of tradition when you go to the theatre. I suppose they are, because you always see them being sold. Anyway, I remember that gardenia, looking like moonlight on my shoulder. The gardenia got all confused with the magic of what was happening on the stage, and I told her that, too.' Livia laughed selfconsciously. 'It's all very silly, I suppose, but it's very nice that she remembered.'

'Another night to change your life,' Maureen said with surprising perception. 'I think it's very sweet.'

'It is,' Livia said softly. 'And it's given me a bit of courage—which I badly need at this point.' She picked up her purse and, still holding the gardenia in her other hand, started for the door. 'I'm going now, before I completely lose my courage. And don't forget to come backstage afterwards. I put your name on the list. And——' she paused for a moment and gave Maureen a tremulous smile, 'thank you for staying with me.'

The doorman was in place, but the backstage regions were silent and dark, except for the two naked bulbs burning at each end of the central corridor. Livia made her way past a series of empty dressing rooms, her footsteps echoing hollowly in the empty building. She started to open her dressing room door and nearly jumped a foot as she heard a noise behind her. She whirled around to find Jonathan's long figure standing in the doorway of his own room.

'I thought I was the first one here,' she said breathlessly.

'No. I have to be early. I can't just dash in at the last minute and jump into character.'

'Nor I,' she agreed quite calmly, because calm—or possibly empty—was the only response he could elicit from her now.

'Livia,' he said slowly, and she bit her lip, staring down at the gardenia in her hand, afraid that he might say something to upset the delicate balance of her life.

'Livia,' he began again, when he realised that she wasn't going to look at him. 'You'll be fine, you know. I haven't any doubts.'

'And you'll be even better,' she said sincerely, and decided that she could chance a look and a slight smile. 'I haven't any doubts either.'

He nodded. 'That's good to hear.' He smiled the crooked smile that had once had the power to move her so. Then he stepped back into his dressing room, and Livia went into hers. The intangible barriers of emotion and the real one of a partition were back in place.

There were two arrangements of flowers on her make-up shelf. One was very formal—from Dickon, she knew without even looking at the card. The other was more casual, a wild display of spring daffodils and iris, with carnations thrown in for scent. The card, each word signed by a different person, simply said, 'Love from the family in the fifth row centre.' With each word in a different hand, it seemed rather to read, 'Love-from-the-family-in-the-fifth-row-centre.'

It was almost a chant, a sort of mantra to hold her together for the first few minutes alone in her dressing room.

Then she could begin to think around the edges of her part and consider, in the most general of terms, some of the things she would have to do before the evening was over. Perhaps the most difficult would be the moment when Jonathan pushed her away. No matter how many times she had done it successfully in rehearsal, she still had visions of losing her balance and crashing down on to the stage floor.

With the thought of Jonathan came the memory of the crooked smile of a few minutes before. That was somehow difficult to handle. That smile was a reminder of the past, when such things had mattered. Even though she had no feeling for him now, there was a sadness in knowing that something once dear to her no longer had the power to move her.

At the proper times, she went through the business of make-up and costume and hair. The half-hour warning was called over the intercom box, and then the fifteen-minute one. Finally she left the dressing room, touching the gardenia for luck, before she went out of the door. Standing in the corridor were a few members of the cast, but no one said anything to her as she made her way towards the stage. There were a few tentative smiles, and she did her best to smile back, although it didn't work well.

It was dim and murky in the wings, almost like a dream world. Nothing was clear and nothing made sense. The vague, shadowy forms of stage hands moved around the edges of the small space. Jonathan stood near the back, recognisable only because of his height. He noticed her, after a minute, and came over.

'How are you?'

'Terrified,' she said quickly, and then forced a smile. 'But I always am, just before I go on.'

'Yes, so am I. I always think opening nights will be the worst, but every night of a run is the same. Opening nights just seem worse when they're happening.'

'I know. I always wonder why I do this for a living, at times like this.'

'That's what makes film so much easier,' he said almost absently. 'You can always do a take-over, if it doesn't come out right the first time. No forgiveness here.'

Livia nodded—not that she knew that much about film—and worried her hands, fingering the wedding band which was a part of her costume. It felt strange on her finger—much too large and very heavy.

'Are you wringing your hands?' Jonathan asked, sounding amused.

'Possibly. I always try to think of something to do, to take my mind off the waiting. I keep trying different things, but none of them work.'

'I count cracks,' Jonathan supplied.

'Cracks in what?'

'Anything that has cracks.' He laughed softly. 'The floor, the ceiling, the wall—you can't imagine what it does to me, when there aren't any cracks.'

'My family sent me flowers, and everyone wrote a different word of the card.' She couldn't imagine why she was telling him this, except that they both had to get through the next few minutes, and talking might be helping, if only slightly. 'It says, "Love from the family in the fifth row centre".'

'Do they expect you to wave?' he asked with humorous disbelief.

'No. Except perhaps when we take our calls. But they always tell me where they're going to be. It goes back to schooldays, when we had pageants and things like that.'

'It's good of you to speak to me,' he said, after a moment's pause. 'I wasn't sure if you ever would again.'

'I expect God and the devil would speak to each other, if they were both waiting to go on stage.'

'And which am I?' he asked with something like a flash of the old amusement.

But before she could answer that, Livia heard the house lights cued down, and then the start of the applause. In an entirely involuntary movement she reached out and grabbed Jonathan's arm, clutching it for dear life in a sudden attack of nerves beyond anything she had ever experienced before.

'It's going to be all right,' he whispered, putting his hand over hers. 'Let's get in place.'

And then he led her on to the stage. They took their places, downstage, just behind the curtain, and then he looked at her without saying a word for what seemed like a very long time.

'Ready?' he asked at last, and she nodded.

He released her hand and she automatically smoothed the fabric of his shirt where she had clung to him.

'All right, then.' He nodded towards the wings and Livia heard, rather than saw, the curtains open.

There was another bit of applause, while they held their places, looking steadily at one another, and then the play began.

It went well. Livia could tell from the beginning that it was going well. A detached part of her could tell such things, just as it could sense the audience listening, and notice when Honey faltered in a line and had to start over. It was that same detached part of her which got her off the stage at the end of each act, down to her dressing room and into the next act's costume, and back up to the wings again.

But never had a part consumed her to the extent that this one did. Never had she felt so totally out of herself, or into herself—she wasn't sure which it was. She had expected to worry, just before Jonathan pushed her away, but she didn't. She was taken by surprise when he actually did it, but her body responded as they had planned, without conscious reaction, and she stumbled across the stage and caught herself in time.

By the last scene she was feeling completely at home in her part. In fact, it wasn't a part any longer. The part was the reality, and she was the pretence. She heard Jonathan begin his final speech, listened to the first few words, and then let her mind slip away.

'There's nothing here any more,' she suddenly heard him say, and looked at him with wonder, because she had heard him say exactly the same thing when it hadn't been a scene in the play. 'There is no second chance—do you understand that? It's over.' He spaced the words with the same bitter venom she had heard from Jonathan—not the man—so recently.

He was looking directly at her, and she shouldn't have been looking back at him. Her mind was supposed to be somewhere else, but she couldn't do it. He was speaking to her, not to the woman. Why hadn't she realised, that awful day, that the words were the same? Now he was saying them for the second time, telling her again that it was over. She knew that all the ragged emotion she had so successfully been keeping at bay was now showing in her face.

'It's over,' he said, giving the curtain line. 'If it was ever real at all.'

She knew she had to wait. She had to hear the curtains close; she had to wait through the brief moment before the applause began. Then she could cry—not for the man and the woman, but for Jonathan and herself—because it was over, and all that they might have meant to one another had been destroyed.

She wiped futilely at her tears. Jonathan was going to see this, she thought in despair—Jonathan and the rest of the cast, and the crew, and, in just a moment, the audience.

And then Jonathan was beside her. 'Livy, Livy, it's all right. I can't think why I'm calling you that; I told you it didn't suit you. I must be a bit unstrung myself, but everything is going to be all right.' He gathered her up in his arms, and as he did so, she caught his brief gesture of delay, directed to the wings.

She leaned against him, burying her face against his shirt, feeling less exposed with his arms around her. With one hand he stroked her hair, and with the other he produced a handkerchief.

'Wipe your eyes,' he commanded. 'We have to take our calls. You can do it. You've done this whole bloody thing, and you can do this.'

He gave her just an instant to dab at her eyes before he called for the curtains to open. Suddenly she was exposed, clutching his handkerchief, with him just a step away and facing her.

He bowed first to her, as though it had been planned. Then he turned to the audience and took her hand, leading her forward so that they could both take their calls. She didn't hear the applause—but then she never had been able to. After a performance, she never heard the applause. She knew she ought to be looking for her family, but she could only grip Jonathan's hand and, without realising it, wipe her eyes again.

That personal gesture, at a time when she ought to be perfectly composed, brought her back to the reality of the moment. It was suddenly imperative that she return the compliment of Jonathan's bow to her. She must somehow let him know how much he had helped.

Her hand still in his, she pivoted, her grey skirt sweeping the floor and draping gracefully as she went down, almost as though she were curtsying to a king. It was appallingly theatrical; she couldn't believe she was doing it. Her free hand swept out, still clutching his handkerchief, involving the audience in her action, and she had done it—as awkward and unnatural as it was.

But Jonathan didn't seem to see it that way. As she looked up again, she saw the appreciative glint in his eye, and the approving smile. She stepped back a pace, and the curtains closed.

'Fifth row centre,' he said in her ear, before the curtains opened again. She found the spot, but only because she could see familiar faces, distinct among the sea of faces. Then, with a commanding gesture, Jonathan summoned the others on to the stage to take their calls.

There were more calls than she could count. She wanted them to end, because her legs were about to give out under her. Once she had thought that endless curtain calls would be the ultimate feeling of glory, something devoutly to be desired. Now they seemed more than she could manage, even if they did seem to indicate a success.

Finally the curtains closed for the last time, and Jonathan took her hand and turned her to face him.

'Are you all right now?'

'Not really,' she said unsteadily. 'If I don't sit down soon, I expect I'll fall.'

He nodded and led her to her chair, upstage. He seemed to be leading her all the time, she thought absently. On to the stage at the start of the play, down for her curtain calls, and now to a chair. It was wrong to be making him do all this—not fair to ask of a man who didn't love you.

She eased gratefully into the chair and felt the tears starting again. 'I'm sorry,' she began, but he didn't appear to be listening. He was looking off towards the wings. Livia followed his gaze and saw the others about to join them.

Jonathan gestured them to stay back, and a very compelling gesture it was, too. 'You're sorry,' he repeated for her. 'But you haven't any reason to be.' He pulled his own chair over to hers and sat down facing her, his face serious. 'I didn't want to do it, you realise—that wretched business at rehearsal, the other day. But you'd suddenly gotten it so awfully wrong——' He paused for an instant, his face looking taut and drawn. 'That was my fault, too. I shouldn't have tried to get us back on the right footing just before the opening. I ought to have left you completely alone last weekend. It was my selfishness—I wanted it all, right then. I shouldn't have expected you to deal with me and the part, all at the same time.' He paused and rubbed his forehead wearily.

'I realised on Monday morning what a mistake I'd made. And I didn't know what to do to correct it. I knew that I had to correct it, though. It wasn't the play, Livia. You have got to believe that. I didn't care about the play any more. It was that damned high ground of yours; I knew we didn't stand a chance, if you didn't manage to get to that high ground of yours. So, I thought perhaps I'd have to use shock tactics.

'You see, all along, that seemed to be the only thing that worked. Whenever you had trouble with the part, I'd get you angry and then you'd get it right. This last time seemed to call for something of the same sort, but I knew it had to be a great deal more extreme. I thought that, if I threw the man's feelings at you—as Livia, not the woman—it might get you back in character. I didn't know what else to do.'

She stared vacantly at him, trying to make sense of his words. 'You didn't mean all those things you said?' she asked at last, feeling the first faint stirrings of hope.

'Of course I didn't mean them,' he answered, as though it were the most obvious thing in the world.

'You only did it to get the right performance out of me,' she said tonelessly, attempting to comprehend what he'd just told her. 'You didn't care about the *play*?' she added on a rising note of incredulity.

'That's right, and I suppose it was worth it. I put you through hell, but you gave the performance of a lifetime—at least what most actors would consider the performance of a lifetime.' He grinned, taking her breath away. 'It did work, although I'd have tried something a little less brutal, if there had been more time.' He grinned again, looking totally pleased with himself. 'Now we've got to see if you can do it six nights a week, with matinees on Wednesdays and Saturdays. Or shall I have to destroy our relationship eight times a week?' He paused and began to hunt through his pockets for a cigarette.

'I hope you haven't got any,' Livia said tartly through her tears. 'It would serve you right!'

'Yes, I know it would. But I rather need something right now.' He found a crumpled pack and took a moment to light a cigarette. 'I've been through my own bit of hell these past few days. I wasn't sure it would turn out right.'

'Do you mean to say that you still weren't sure I'd get the part right?' she demanded.

'Lord, no—I had no doubts about that. What had me worried was whether you'd ever forgive me—or even give me a chance to explain all this. But I got a faint glimmer of hope when you looked at me with such a marvellously haunted expression, at the very end of the play. I decided that you might not have forgiven me, but at least you cared, if only a little.' Jonathan paused for a moment, eyes narrowed consideringly. 'That was a very good piece of work—that expression. I can't think why it didn't occur to me to have you use it. As the director, it ought to have. It makes a completely different play out of it, you know. It gives——'

'Jonathan,' she said firmly, cutting him off, 'I don't give a damn about the play right now.'

'Sorry,' he grinned engagingly. 'I don't either, actually. I've gotten rather off the track, haven't I? I was about to find out if you've forgiven me for that rather brutal piece of direction.'

'I don't think there's anything to forgive,' she said carefully. 'As you said, there wasn't time for anything else. Besides, it worked, didn't it?'

He leaned back in his chair, looking remarkably satisfied. 'Then you will marry me.'

It was a statement, not a question, and Livia frowned. 'You might at least have asked me! But I will, anyway.'

'As soon as possible? I'll give you that one as a question.'

'As soon as possible.' She nodded solemnly and then, with a return of humour, she added, 'If you'll just give me time to run out to the fifth row centre, and tell my family what's going to happen.'

'Oh, they'll be backstage with everyone else by now,' Jonathan said airily. 'And your mother already knows, although she promised not to tell the rest until you knew.'

'How does my mother happen to know?' Livia demanded, delighting in his satisfied smile and the way years and cares seemed to have fallen away from him.

'Well, I called her, to see what flowers I should send—what would mean the most to you. And I found myself explaining rather more to her than I'd intended. She inspires confidences, doesn't she?'

'Yes, she really does,' Livia agreed, before the rest of what he had said sunk in. '*You* sent the gardenia!' she whispered, and began to cry again. 'I thought she had.'

'She told me a gardenia would mean the most, especially as I was planning to marry you, if you'd have me. Of course, when I talked to her, there was considerable doubt about that—all of which I explained to her. And she made me feel quite a bit better. She told me that you're basically a forgiving soul, which was good to hear. But she also told me how reasonable you are and—since I'd had plenty of opportunity to see how totally wrong she is about *that*—I did wonder how much reliance I really ought to put in anything she had to say. But——' and here he paused, seeing Livia about to explode, and then said hastily, 'you're about to prove my point, Livia dear, and make a liar of your mother, and I don't think that either of us really wants to do that. I'll switch deftly back to the gardenia, because that seems to bring out the better side of your nature.' And then he paused again to simply stare at her with an arrested and thoroughly delighted expression.

'Your mother said——' he began at length, appearing to have a little difficulty in picking up the thread of his thought, 'she said that you'd know what I meant by the gardenia, even if I didn't, and still don't, for that matter. Look, don't go crying again,' he instructed, in a sudden shift. 'And you can tell me what the gardenia means later. We've got people stacked up like cordwood in the wings—all waiting to tell us what a wonderful job we've done. I'd rather they didn't see you totally smeared and streaked. I do believe you're a star—or will be after the reviews come out. You don't need to marry me now, you know,' he added almost anxiously. 'You can pretty well do exactly what you want to do, after this night's work.'

'I want to marry you,' Livia said firmly, dabbing at her eyes.

'Yes, but you've got the high ground, you know. No need to fight for it any longer. It's yours, and you can do what you please with it. Perhaps you'd rather be there alone.'

'You're the one who suggested there might be room for both of us up here. I rather like the idea,' she added almost shyly.

'Well,' Jonathan expelled a sigh, 'that's settled, then. Thank God!' He stood up, pulling her to her feet and then folding her into his arms. 'Thank you, Livia,' he said carefully, one hand absently smoothing back her hair. 'This has been hell, you know. I didn't know what would happen if I ruined everything. I was pretty sure there would be other chances for you, but I knew there wouldn't be any more for me. You were my last chance, Livia—that much, at least, I did know.' Then he kissed her with abrupt passion, before setting her back on her feet. 'Come along,' he directed in a more normal tone, 'you've got to meet your admiring public, and I'd rather like to meet your family. I've got something to say to them, you know.'

Livia was sure that he did have something to say to them—quite a lot, probably, because Jonathan always did have quite a lot to say to anyone. She wasn't sure, though, exactly what it was that he would say to them because—given Jonathan—anything was possible.

He led her back into the wings, where they were immediately surrounded by the first of the well-wishers. The two of them slowly made their way down the stairs to their dressing rooms, meeting many of Jonathan's friends, and a surprising number of Livia's, too. It was hard to speak because there was too much noise and too many competing claims. But Dickon managed to get through long enough to shake Jonathan's hand and then give Livia a quick hug.

'I was wrong, wasn't I?' he shouted in her ear, and then managed a benign smile, when she nodded wordlessly.

They moved past Perry, who wore a satisfied and all-knowing grin, and he gave Livia a happy, thumbs-up gesture as they moved by. Maureen materialised long enough to call out, 'I don't think you need to explain, Livy.'

'I know,' Livia shouted back, 'and I'll introduce you, soon.'

Finally, just outside her dressing room door, Livia saw her family. With the exception of her mother, they all looked a bit dazed and thoroughly out of their element. Livia's mother, on the other hand, appeared to feel quite at home, and she, too, was wearing a knowing smile.

'Here they are,' Livia explained to Jonathan, when she had the opportunity. 'My parents, and my uncles and aunts, and some of my cousins—most of them, actually.'

'The ones who were there at Christmas time?' he asked, and she nodded.

He smiled his most charming smile and swept everyone into Livia's dressing room, where there was slightly more room and a bit less noise. He even accomplished the introductions, commanding the situation to such an extent that everyone—except Livia's mother—looked thoroughly bemused.

He was patient for a time, accepting the tentative compliments directed to him and allowing their more enthusiastic words for Livia. But he was clearly straining at the lead, wanting to get to what he considered the important business at hand.

Finally, at the first hint of a lull, he captured their attention, casting a quick glance at Livia as he silenced them with a gesture.

'Do you remember that strange call Livia got, back at Christmas time—the one that came in the middle of the night? It was the one where she had nothing to say, except a lot of yeses and noes—which is totally unlike Livia, you must admit. Do you remember it?' he demanded, wanting a response from them, and not getting it.

Eventually there were a few rather confused nods, not because they didn't remember the call, but because they didn't quite see what it had to do with the events of the evening.

'Well,' Jonathan continued with relish, smiling delightedly down at Livia, while her breath caught and she looked fondly back at him, 'she didn't want to tell you—although I said she ought to—but I was calling to ask her to marry me.'

There was a moment's silence, while they attempted to digest this rather unorthodox announcement. Then

Karen, always the most irrepressible of the cousins, spoke up.

'I told you, that very night, Livy, that he was sweet on you,' she said reproachfully. 'But you said he was too flamboyant for your taste.'

'Oh, I am, undoubtedly,' Jonathan agreed cheerfully. 'That's what makes it all so interesting. But actually, I think Livia's made great progress, since Christmas. And so,' he added on a more thoughtful note, smiling down at Livia, 'have I.'

And with that observation Livia could heartily agree, she decided, as their eyes met and she smiled confidently back at him.

BOOK MATE PLUS®

The perfect companion for all larger books! Use it to hold open cookbooks... or while reading in bed or tub. Books stay open flat, or prop upright on an easellike base... pages turn without removing see-through strap. And pockets for notes and pads let it double as a handy portfolio!

**17" x 11" OPEN.
SNAPS SHUT
TO 8½" x 11".**

Only $9.95 each— order yours today!

Available now. Send your name, address, and zip or postal code, along with a check or money order for just $9.95, plus 75¢ for postage and handling, for a total of $10.70 (New York & Arizona residents add appropriate sales tax) payable to Harlequin Reader Service to:

Harlequin Reader Service

In U.S.
P.O. Box 52040
Phoenix, AZ 85072-9988

In Canada
649 Ontario Street
Stratford, Ont. N5A 6W2